ESCAPE
TO MURRAY
RIVER

Books by Robert Elmer

ADVENTURES DOWN UNDER

#1 / *Escape to Murray River*
#2 / *Captive at Kangaroo Springs*
#3 / *Rescue at Boomerang Bend*
#4 / *Dingo Creek Challenge*
#5 / *Race to Wallaby Bay*

THE YOUNG UNDERGROUND

#1 / *A Way Through the Sea*
#2 / *Beyond the River*
#3 / *Into the Flames*
#4 / *Far From the Storm*
#5 / *Chasing the Wind*
#6 / *A Light in the Castle*
#7 / *Follow the Star*
#8 / *Touch the Sky*

ESCAPE TO MURRAY RIVER

BETHANY HOUSE PUBLISHERS
MINNEAPOLIS, MINNESOTA 55438

Escape to Murray River
Copyright © 1997
Robert Elmer

Cover illustration by Chris Ellison
Cover design by Peter Glöege

Published by Bethany House Publishers
A Ministry of Bethany Fellowship International
11300 Hampshire Avenue South
Minneapolis, Minnesota 55438

Printed in the United States of America by
Bethany Press International, Minneapolis, Minnesota 55438

Library of Congress Cataloging-in-Publication Data

Elmer, Robert.
　　Escape to Murray River / by Robert Elmer.
　　　　p.　cm. — (Adventures down under ; 1)
　　Summary: In 1868, after their father is wrongfully convicted and deported on the last prison ship to Australia, twelve-year-old Patrick and the rest of the McWaid family determine to stay together and follow him to the far-off continent.
　　ISBN 1–55661–923–5 (pbk.)
　　[1. Family life—Ireland—Fiction. 2. Ireland—Fiction. 3. Voyages and travel—Fiction. 4. Australia—Fiction.] I. Title. II. Series: Elmer, Robert. Adventures down under ; 1.
PZ7.E4794Es　　1997
[Fic]—dc21

97–21034
CIP
AC

To Ron and Robin:

Godly examples, heroes, and friends.

MEET ROBERT ELMER

ROBERT ELMER is the author of THE YOUNG UNDERGROUND series, as well as many magazine and newspaper articles. He lives with his wife, Ronda, and their three children, Kai, Danica, and Stefan (and their dog, Freckles) in a Washington State farming community just a bike ride away from the Canadian border.

CONTENTS

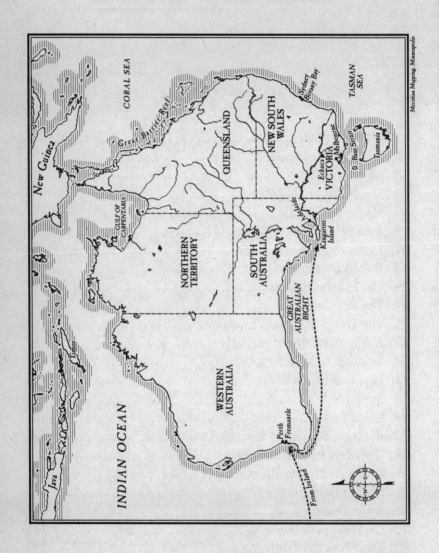

INDIAN OCEAN

New Guinea

CORAL SEA

Great Barrier Reef

GULF OF
CARPENTARIA

Java

Timor

QUEENSLAND

NEW SOUTH
WALES

Sydney
Botany Bay

TASMAN
SEA

NORTHERN
TERRITORY

SOUTH
AUSTRALIA

Adelaide

Echuca
VICTORIA
Melbourne

Bass Strait

Tasmania

Kangaroo
Island

WESTERN
AUSTRALIA

GREAT
AUSTRALIAN
BIGHT

Perth
Fremantle

From Ireland

Meridian Mapping, Minneapolis

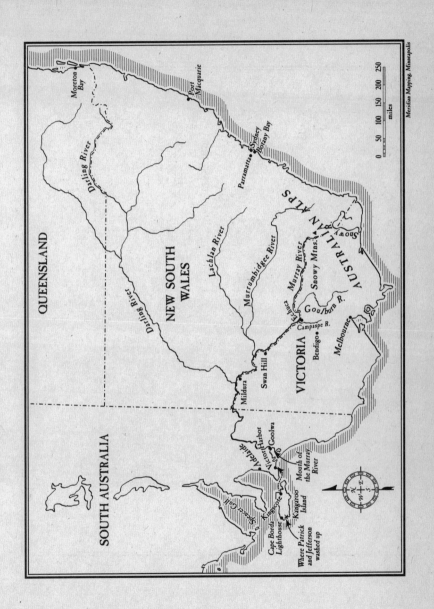

QUEENSLAND

NEW SOUTH WALES

SOUTH AUSTRALIA

VICTORIA

AUSTRALIAN ALPS

Morton Bay

Darling River

Port Macquarie

Parramatta

Sydney

Botany Bay

Lachlan River

Murrumbidgee River

Darling River

Snowy Mtns.

Snowy R.

Murray River

Echuca

Goulburn R.

Campaspe R.

Bendigo

Melbourne

Swan Hill

Mildura

Spencer Gulf

Adelaide

Victor Harbor

Goolwa

Mouth of the Murray River

Kangaroo Island

Kingscote

Cape Borda Lighthouse

Where Patrick and Jefferson washed up

Meridian Mapping, Minneapolis

0   50   100   150   200   250
miles

N
W   E
S

CHAPTER 1

AFTERNOON SPIES

"Michael! We're going to be late if you don't stay by me."

Twelve-year-old Patrick McWaid put his hands on his hips and waited yet again for his younger brother to catch up. They had come this way hundreds of times before, through Dublin's Bull Alley Market, and it was the quickest way from the flat where they lived to their father's newspaper office on the other side of the River Liffey. But Patrick's little brother, Michael, was dawdling as usual.

"I'm coming, Patrick."

If they had the money, they could have bought nearly anything from a vendor on the crowded market street. Prayer books or pig's cheeks, candles, onions, secondhand clothes, wallpaper, or maybe even American bacon. Patrick's eight-year-old brother had stopped to inspect a rabbit displayed on a board, ready for someone's dinner. He rubbed his button nose and sniffed sadly.

"Poor bunny," whispered Michael, wrinkling his forehead. "If he were alive . . ."

An old lady bumped into Patrick from behind with her cart, and he could tell right away from the smell what was inside.

"Dublin Bay Her-r-in'!" shrieked the woman as Patrick jumped out of her way. He knew better than to challenge a Dublin fishmonger. She was one in an army of women who sold the silvery hand-sized herring that were hauled in every day from the Irish Sea.

"Ripe plums," announced a young girl sitting on the pavement. Patrick knew without looking that she would be as ragged and dirty looking as the rest of the children sent out on the streets to sell fruit. "Red as your hair, boy. Ten for a penny!"

Patrick was used to people teasing him about his short-cropped red hair, his rather large ears, and his freckles, so he wasn't upset as he grabbed his brother's wrist and tried to drag him away from the meat merchant's handcart. He just thought he'd better leave before he spent the money in his pocket.

Besides, in the early August morning, the handcart smelled even worse than the fish woman's cart, and it was already covered in flies. The summer of 1867 was warm for Ireland.

"We didn't come this way to stare at rabbit skins, Michael, and I don't believe it would make a very good pet for your collection, being dead."

But Michael only looked up at his big brother with questions in his large, dark eyes. "You always used to like to come here and look, Patrick. How come you're so grumpy today?"

For a moment Patrick felt guilty at his brother's question, and he closed his eyes to think of an answer. He hadn't meant to be upset, only . . .

"Buy a box of matches from this poor, old blind woman," sang another voice, and Patrick snapped open his eyes to see the empty stare and half grin of the aging match seller. The boys had grown up hearing her cry; she lived on the street from early morning until midnight, every day except Sunday. Today, Patrick and Michael hurried without another word past the blind woman's station on the corner.

"Sorry, Michael," Patrick finally told his brother. "I just didn't want to lose you in the market."

Michael ran on ahead. "All right, then. I'll race you to the River Liffey. First one to the Wellington Bridge—"

"No!" Patrick shouted so loudly that a woman hanging her laundry out a fifth-floor window above stopped what she was doing to stare. Michael froze in his tracks.

"I told you before, we are *not* going over the Wellington Bridge." Patrick didn't want to explain his reason to his younger brother.

12

"We'll go over O'Connell Bridge, where there are more people."

"But that's a longer walk. I thought you were in a hurry."

Patrick hoped to keep his shoes clean as they passed behind a horse-drawn wagon loaded down with beer barrels. With so many horses and very few street cleaners . . .

"I don't care. We're not going over the Wellington Bridge. Not ever again."

"But why not?"

Patrick didn't answer, but he couldn't keep the picture of the bridge out of his mind, the memory of how their youngest brother, Sean, had drowned. The same memory had haunted him for more than a year, and it flashed over and over in his mind. Odd as it seemed, he couldn't describe the accident to Michael—or to his parents, either. He had tried once to tell his older sister, Becky, but he wasn't sure she understood.

It was my fault, he blamed himself again, as he had every time he remembered. *If only I hadn't let him play on the bridge railing. If only . . .*

Even without closing his eyes he could see again how Sean had lost his balance, waving his arms and falling backward off the bridge railing. Patrick reached out too late—then Sean was gone. Not even the policeman who happened by could reach his brother in time.

"It wasn't your fault," the policeman had said. Patrick's older sister had said the same thing. But nothing made him feel better.

But it was *my fault*, he argued. *My fault—and the river's*.

Of course that made no sense at all, so he kept his fears bottled away. To make sure they didn't pour out, he promised himself never to return to the spot where Sean had drowned. Not now. Not ever. Problem was, even the sight of water brought the memories back.

"Patrick!" Michael waved him over to an organ-grinder's cart near the side of the street, just around the corner from their father's office on Middle Abbey Street. The bouncy melody was out of tune, but Patrick had to smile. Michael had found another animal.

"Here, fella," whispered Michael, edging closer to the organ-grinder's little monkey, perched on the man's shoulder. On a chain leash, the nervous animal was dressed in a red military coat, blue-braided trousers, and a pillbox hat. He held a small tin cup, rattling a couple of shillings to catch the attention of gentlemen passing by in tall black hats and ladies carrying frilly-edged umbrellas.

"I want to get a monkey like that someday, Patrick."

"Maybe when you're running your own zoological gardens. But right now we'd better get to Pa's office for lunch, or he's going to be wondering what happened to us."

Patrick turned to go, then felt the coin his father had left him before he went to work that morning. A halfpenny. Maybe enough to buy a handful of plums or a few pieces of rock candy. Before he could think again about the treat, he turned and gave the coin to his brother.

"Give it to the monkey, Michael."

Michael grinned and held the coin up for the animal to see, then giggled as the monkey jumped to his shoulder to collect the reward.

"And what song do you boys want to hear, eh?" The organ-grinder flashed them a toothy grin, looking pleased at their small donation. "How about 'Has Anybody Here Seen Kelly?' " He cranked his organ with new energy, and the odd instrument wheezed and groaned to life.

The *Freeman's Journal* and the *Evening Telegraph* were both published in the same large, rambling offices that took up a four-story brick building on Middle Abbey Street. Like the rest of Dublin, the building was crafted of speckled brick, from rusty brown to sandy yellow.

"Well, good day to you, boys." The man sitting at the front desk gave them a smile when they pushed open the heavy front door to stand awkwardly in the lobby. He twirled the handle of his long black moustache and pointed through an open doorway. "You'll be looking for your pa—unless you came to visit me?"

"Hello, Mr. Hogan. We're going to eat lunch with him today."

"Lucky lads. You know where his office is."

"Thank you, sir."

Michael kept in close step behind Patrick as they threaded their way through the busy office full of reporters, editors, and errand boys. One of the boys, dropping a stack of papers on a desk, turned to look at them when they entered the room.

"Hey, Patrick. Any news?"

"I don't know." Patrick had traded greetings with him before. "Thought you'd be able to tell me."

The older boy chuckled as he hurried away. "Your father's down the hall talking to someone," he told them. "You better wait in his office."

Patrick didn't mind waiting. His father's glass-walled office was small, but Patrick thought it was very important looking. He ran his finger over the engraved letters of the brass nameplate resting on the edge of the large mahogany desk—J.M. McWaid, Senior Correspondent—then found a place to sit on the floor.

"Hide back here with me," suggested Michael, sliding behind and underneath the desk. "Then when Pa comes . . ."

"Okay, okay." They had played this game before, and their father still always pretended to be surprised.

"Hold your breath," whispered Michael, holding back a giggle. "I think he's coming."

They heard footsteps by the door—more than one set.

"See him?" asked a gruff-sounding man, a voice Patrick didn't recognize. Patrick held his breath and tried to pull his toes out of view.

"I told you, Inspector, I sent him off for at least a half hour," replied another man. Conrad Burke—their father's boss.

"Perfect." The inspector, whoever that might have been, laughed quietly. They stepped inside the office, and someone shut the door. "You're learning this business more quickly than I thought."

Patrick wasn't sure what "business" they were talking about, and he wondered why the two men were in his father's office. He held Michael tightly to keep his younger brother from squirming.

"As long as you keep your end—" Burke didn't sound so sure.

"Oh, now don't worry about your money," interrupted the other man. "When this is all over, you'll be a rich man. It's just a shame about your reporter." His voice didn't make it sound as if he thought it was a shame at all.

"You said yourself he's too curious for his own good. He's too close. I'm sure he knows."

"Oh, he does, and I can see the headlines now: 'Chief Police Inspector Caught in Bribery Scandal.'"

"Not in this newspaper, Inspector. I already told you. This will put him away. No one is going to believe a word of what McWaid says. Not after this."

"Yes, yes—you've told me that before. Now put the money there in the drawer, and we'll be done with it. Do you remember what to say?"

Burke mumbled something, and Patrick heard the drawer next to them yanked open.

How can he not see us? thought Patrick as he pulled his brother back even farther into the shadow of the desk. He thought he would almost suffocate Michael, his arm was so tight around his younger brother's shoulder.

"A rotten business, but someone has to do it," Burke said as the pair walked out. Everything was now quiet, but the brothers remained in their hiding place, shivering.

"Are they gone?" Michael whispered after nearly five minutes had passed.

Slowly, gently, Patrick unfolded his cramped legs and slipped out of their hiding place. He peeked over the desk to make sure.

"They're gone."

"But what were they doing here? Who were they?"

"One of them was Pa's boss, Mr. Burke. He was the one who put something in the desk. The other man . . . did you hear what Mr. Burke called him?"

"Inspector. That's a kind of chief of police, isn't it?"

"I think so. I just don't know what they were doing here in Pa's office."

Michael shrugged his shoulders. "I remember what they said, but I don't know what it means."

Patrick carefully checked the quiet hallway. "My brother, the boy who remembers everything."

"I can't help it, Patrick. Things just stick in my head."

"I know." Patrick looked out again, and a man ran past.

"Let's see what's going on," said Patrick as he hurried after the man.

The main office was in chaos. Everyone was out of his desk, standing in a knot around a tall, handsome man with a powerful build, hazel eyes, and curly red hair—Patrick and Michael's father. He had to stoop down to stand face-to-face with a small, portly man who held an unlit cigar between his lips. Two uniformed policemen stood by, looking bored, and the man in charge had the smug look of someone who knew what was going to happen next. He crossed his arms and leaned back on his heels.

"Well, if you've nothing to hide, Mr. McWaid, then I'm sure you'll have nothing against my men taking a look through your office, just to check on things."

As soon as the man spoke, Patrick knew who it was. The chief inspector!

"Pa!" Michael rushed headfirst into the crowd. "We've been looking for you."

Patrick's father looked around when he heard the voice of his youngest son, and his eyes locked with Patrick's for a moment. He held up his large hand as he passed by with the police inspector and his officers.

"I'm sorry, boys. This will just take a minute, and then we'll go out to lunch."

"Hear, hear—what's going on?" Conrad Burke swept into the room with an armful of papers. He nervously combed the wispy black hair away from his high forehead, and his jet-black eyes darted around the room. "What's the meaning of this?"

The police inspector paused for a moment and gave a slight bow at the sight of the *Evening Telegraph*'s managing editor.

"Begging your pardon, sir." There was a flicker of a grin on the man's face, but only a flicker. "But we'll be out of your way in just a moment. I'm Chief Inspector Mahoney, city police." He stuck out his hand.

"Yes, of course, Chief Inspector." Burke didn't smile. "A pleasure to finally meet you. But here?"

Finally? thought Patrick. *These men are good actors.*

"As I said," the inspector went on, "I apologize for the intrusion. But we must take every tip seriously. And we have a source who tells us that your Mr. McWaid is a key member of the Fenians."

At that, Patrick's father burst out laughing, then covered his mouth. "Oh, so that's what this is all about, is it? Well, forgive me for saying so, sir, but I'm no more a Fenian than you are an Indian chief."

"What's a Fenian, Pa?" asked Michael as they walked back toward their father's office.

Patrick answered for his father. "They're a rebel group. It's against the law to be a part of them because they're against the government."

"That's all?"

"Not really," said their father. "You go to prison if anyone thinks you're a member. The Fenians want Ireland to be free from England, and the things they'll do for independence can hurt other people."

Michael nodded as though he understood. By that time the two uniformed officers were searching the office where Patrick and Michael had been hiding minutes before. They looked behind pictures, under chairs, and through papers on the large desk. One pulled a bulging envelope from a desk drawer. When he opened it, money fluttered to the office floor, hushing everyone into a shocked silence.

"Ah, Mr. McWaid," said the police inspector, strolling over to pick up a bill. He fingered the one-hundred-pound note and looked at Patrick's father. "Looks as if you're saving a considerable sum of money here in your drawer. Planning to buy a country house, perhaps?"

Mr. McWaid's face clouded, and he rushed to his desk. "I've never seen this money before in my life!"

But the inspector's cold eyes didn't blink. The officer handed him the envelope, and he pulled out a note and read, " 'John, here's the first part of the advance. More to come at our next meeting. Seamus.' "

"I have no idea what this is about," sputtered Mr. McWaid. His face was red with fury as two policemen stepped up to hold him by the arms, as if they had practiced the move. "Someone must have hidden that envelope there!"

The inspector nodded politely and smiled as he handed the envelope over to Burke. "Seamus. That wouldn't be Seamus Kelly, the Fenian gangster, now, would it? Why would such a ruffian be writing notes and passing along such a sum of money to a respectable newspaper reporter like John McWaid?"

"I'm telling you, I have no idea where this . . . this money came from." Patrick's father tried to pull his arms forward, but he was held firmly. "I've never seen that money or that envelope before, and I have no connections with Kelly."

"You let him go!" insisted Michael, but a gentle look from their father kept him back.

"It's all right, Michael," Mr. McWaid reassured him. "It's just a misunderstanding."

"It must be a misunderstanding, Chief . . . what did you say your name was?" Burke turned to the police officer.

"Mahoney, sir. Chief Inspector Mahoney. And, aye, sir, I hope it is just that." He gave Burke a slight nod as he took the envelope full of money and slipped it into the pocket of his tweed jacket. "But with this kind of evidence, you understand we'll need to question your man further at the station."

"Pa!" Patrick couldn't help crying out when one of the policemen began leading his father out the door. "It's not right!" Without thinking, he grabbed for his father's arm, but he was shoved to the floor by one of the officers.

"Hey, now, there's no need for that!" protested Mr. McWaid. He stopped to look back at his sons as the policemen parted a way through the crowd that had gathered in front of the door. But there was nothing he could do.

"All right, everyone," growled Burke. "Show's over." He cleared his throat and looked at the floor as Patrick's father was led past him. "Ah . . . look, McWaid, we'll do our best to get this . . . ah, misunderstanding cleared up."

Michael helped his brother to his feet as their father was led out of the building. The tears stung at Patrick's eyes.

"I'm sorry about lunch." Patrick's father tried to comfort his boys. "But tell your ma I'll be home for dinner. It's all a terrible mistake."

Patrick and Michael could only follow down the hallways and out the building while Inspector Mahoney and his men led their father into the back of a black covered police wagon.

"Boys!" Mr. Burke called to them from the office door, but Patrick wouldn't listen. He stared up at the barred window at the back of the wagon. When the driver put his two chocolate brown draft horses into a trot, the boys ran along behind. They kept up for several blocks, until Michael stumbled on an uneven cobblestone and skinned his knee.

"We're not helping him by standing here crying in the street," Patrick managed between breaths. He looked at Michael, knowing that the tears in his brother's eyes were like his own—and not from the skinned knee.

"B-but, Patrick . . ."

They watched as the wagon disappeared around a corner, and Patrick tried to wipe away his tears with a sleeve. This wasn't supposed to have happened. Not today, not ever. But everything about the past hour was so confusing. The men talking in his father's office. The arrest. The way the police inspector and Conrad Burke had acted.

"Did you see Mr. Burke?" asked Patrick. "He pretended he had never met the police inspector."

"But they were talking in Pa's office before—"

"And Mr. Burke put something in Pa's drawer. He put that money there to make people think Pa had hidden it!"

A ROTTEN BUSINESS

"Boys, boys." Sarah McWaid put her hands on her sons' shoulders and smiled patiently. "Take a breath and start over. I cannot understand a single word you've said."

"But, Ma, they were mean to him!" cried Michael, and Patrick spilled out their story once more, as clearly as he could manage. His mother's clear green eyes widened as the words hit her.

"Did the bullies from Bull Alley follow you again?" Their fourteen-year-old sister stepped into the main living room from the kitchen, wiping her hands on an apron. Her full name was Rebecca Elisabeth McWaid, but their father had always called her "Becky" and told her she was the prettiest lass in all of Dublin—though Patrick thought this might be stretching things a bit. Despite what Patrick thought, however, Becky did attract the attention of most of the boys in the neighborhood, with her wavy nut brown hair, petite good looks, and sparkling eyes that always seemed to laugh when she talked. But her smile froze now at the sight of both brothers in tears.

". . . and then they took him away in the police wagon," finished Michael.

Mrs. McWaid sank into one of their comfortable reading chairs, taking hold of Patrick's hand.

"Now, tell me again . . . you're certain it was Mr. Burke and

Chief Inspector Mahoney in your pa's office? And what exactly were they saying?"

"It was Pa's boss and the police inspector, Ma. I'm sure of that."

"Burke said, 'It's a rotten business,'" added Michael, using a deep voice for effect.

Snatches of the odd conversation came back to Patrick and he nodded. "First the inspector said something about 'the reporter'—he must have meant Pa—was getting too close . . . that he didn't want him to find out about something bad."

"What's a bridalry scandal, Ma?" asked Michael.

"Where did you hear that?"

"That's what the inspector said he was afraid of."

"No, it was *bribery*," Patrick corrected him. "I think maybe someone is paying him money to do something wrong, and he doesn't want anyone to find out."

"Bribery?" Becky wasn't following what her brothers were trying to say, and neither was their mother.

"I didn't understand all they were saying, either, Becky, but sure enough Burke put something in Pa's drawer. An envelope full of money. And a phony note."

"But why?" Mrs. McWaid looked at her three children. "And how could they accuse your father of being in with the Fenians? He could be sent to prison."

"He *is* in prison, Ma," answered Patrick.

"No, I mean for a long time."

"What's going to happen, Ma?" Becky had knotted the towel in her hands.

Mrs. McWaid set her jaw and sat up straight. "We're going to—"

She was interrupted by an urgent rap on the door. Patrick nearly jumped out of his shirt.

"Who's that?" Michael sniffled and wiped his nose on his sleeve.

"Mrs. McWaid? Are you there, Mrs. McWaid?" It was the muffled but unmistakable voice of the last man in the world Patrick wanted to see just then.

"Open the door, would you please, Patrick?" Their mother rose quickly and straightened her apron and auburn hair.

Patrick could only stare at his mother, frozen in place. "But it's *him*," he hissed.

She put a finger to her lips and gave him a warning with her eyes. Like her daughter, Becky, she was petite and slender, but completely in charge.

Patrick unlocked the door.

"Oh, there you are, my boy." Mr. Burke looked in curiously. "I was worried about you and your brother."

Patrick had an almost irresistible urge to slam the door in the man's face. Instead, he backed away from Mr. Burke's hard gaze.

"May I come in?"

"Yes, of course, Mr. Burke." Patrick's mother sounded as if she were inviting a good friend in for tea. "Please do."

Burke held his black top hat in his hand and stepped into the front room. He had been there only once before; Patrick couldn't quite remember when. Maybe when Pa had been promoted to senior writer for the newspaper. Now Mr. Burke stood in the entry, a horrible, twisted look on his face, the bearer of bad news.

"The boys have told you what happened at the office, no doubt?"

"Yes, Mr. Burke. Please sit down. Patrick, you'll take his hat?"

And stomp it flat, thought Patrick, but he nodded and obeyed.

Mr. Burke sat on the edge of a sofa, nervously recounting the story—the complete surprise of the arrest, the rude behavior of the police, his own desperate efforts to stop what was happening. He mopped his high, glistening forehead with a handkerchief.

"I'll tell you, Mrs. McWaid, it was an astonishing surprise. I did my best to explain to the gentlemen that there was some kind of terrible mistake, but no one would listen. . . ."

Patrick's mother nodded politely and pressed her thin lips together tightly as Burke continued.

"My own opinion of the matter is they will discover very quickly that they have the wrong man, and your husband will be home for dinner, his name cleared."

"We heard you talking in my pa's office!" Michael blurted out without warning. The room was quiet except for the ticking of the mantel clock, and Mr. Burke searched the room, his eyebrows knit tightly over his deep-set black eyes.

"What was that, lad?" This time the man's words were a challenge as he found and then stared directly at Michael. Patrick's little brother glanced down at the floor. "I said we heard you talking in my pa's office." Michael crossed his arms as if that settled everything. Patrick could hear his own heart, beating louder than the mantel clock.

"And where might you have been? In the hallway, perhaps?"

"No, we were hiding under the desk. We heard everything you said to the inspector."

Patrick wanted to kick his little brother to get him to stop, but he was across the room.

Burke rubbed his cheeks thoughtfully, but he seemed unconcerned.

"Then, you heard me tell the inspector I didn't think your father was the man he was looking for, did you not?" Burke seemed to have an answer for everything. And almost like a hypnotist, he was trying to make them believe things had happened that really hadn't.

Patrick didn't remember it that way. *He's trying to find out what we heard.*

"We saw you put something in his desk."

This time Patrick thought he saw Mr. Burke's jaw stiffen—but only slightly.

"You did, did you? You're an observant lad, even when you're hiding under your pa's desk." He laughed and patted Michael on the head, then cleared his throat. "It was a story your father and I were working on. Just some papers, I'm afraid."

Patrick tried to remember again what Mr. Burke had been saying while he was in their father's office.

"But truly, lad, if you want to see your father again, you'll sure not to repeat a story of that sort. Leave it to me, and I'll do my best to have your father freed."

Patrick's eyes narrowed. He was sure he had seen Mr. Burke squirm in fear, if only for a moment.

"Now, Mrs. McWaid, as I said, I'm hoping your husband will be released tonight." Mr. Burke stood and took back his hat. "And I want you to know that I'm doing everything within my power to have John's name cleared." He twirled his hat in his hand and backed away toward the door. For a moment Patrick had his back turned to the man, and he felt a painful grip take his shoulders.

"Remember, lad—I'm just as shocked and upset by this as you must be."

Then he was gone, and Mrs. McWaid leaned on the door as she bolted it shut.

"He's lying, Ma." Patrick rubbed his shoulders.

Becky only frowned. "You don't know that for certain, Patrick," his sister told him.

"But we were there," he argued.

"Ma, what do you think?" Michael asked.

Mrs. McWaid didn't answer, didn't even turn around. She only buried her face in her arms and cried quietly, her shoulders shaking.

Patrick bit his lip. "I'm sorry, Ma." He put his arms around her shoulders and patted her on the back. "I wish we could do something."

Michael slipped in between the door and his mother, catching a couple of her tears on his dark, wavy hair before wrapping his own arms around her. Becky squeezed in close, too.

"No, I'm the one who's sorry, children." Mrs. McWaid choked back another sob. "It's just . . ."

"It's just not right," finished Patrick. "That Mr. Burke, I'd like to tell him a thing or two."

"Now, wait a minute." Their mother took a deep breath and stood up straight, still holding on to them. "We don't know the entire story yet, now, do we?"

No one answered, and Patrick thought back to the strange events of the afternoon. Everything had gone wrong, and now his father was gone. And Mr. Burke, well, he wasn't sure what to think of Mr. Burke anymore.

"Nothing makes sense, Ma," Becky finally whispered. "Why would someone say all those lies about Pa?"

"I don't know." Mrs. McWaid shook her head, then closed her eyes and looked down at the floor.

Patrick wasn't sure how long they stood there, but they prayed, taking turns like they did before a meal or at bedtime. This time it was different, though, because no one hurried to finish, not even Michael. At last they opened their eyes, and Mrs. McWaid went to fill a washbasin.

"Get yourselves cleaned up," she told them. "We're going to find your father and bring him home."

CHAPTER 3

ALL LIES

Patrick wished he could disappear into the carved wood paneling of the Dublin courtroom. He hadn't meant to shout; it had just slipped out when he saw his father led through the doors in chains.

"One more outburst like that, young man," thundered the white-wigged judge, "and I shall have you removed!"

"Shh, Patrick," warned Mrs. McWaid.

Like Patrick, she hadn't seen John McWaid at all in the past several weeks, ever since the awful day of the arrest. Not because they hadn't tried, but nothing they said that day or since could convince the jailers to let them visit Mr. McWaid.

"I've my orders, ma'am," the guard had told her with a blank expression. "No visitors for McWaid."

Now she only held Patrick back with a tired, quivering hand. Becky and Michael just stared, horrified, as their father found his seat on a plain wooden bench at the front of the courtroom. His eyes looked hollow and sunken, but for a moment he glanced in their direction, and Patrick thought he saw him smile weakly. A uniformed policeman with a double-breasted jacket and a tall, rounded helmet crossed his arms and looked bored.

"I'm sorry," Patrick mouthed the words. His throat had closed so tightly that he could hardly breathe, much less shout.

Hiding behind the folds of his tentlike black robe, His Honor, Justice Sir Harold S. Dalrymple, peered over the rims of his spectacles to a pile of papers on the counter before him.

The rest of the trial passed as if in a bad dream. His father's simple words fell empty before another man in a wig, pacing in front of the judge's tall desk.

"Why don't they believe him, Ma?" whispered Michael, and his mother put a finger to her lips.

"Shh, or they'll throw us out."

"You say you have no knowledge of how this note came to be found in your desk?" The prosecutor waved a piece of paper in the air in front of Mr. McWaid.

"No, sir," began Patrick's father. "As I've said . . ."

The trial dragged on that way, with the stern-looking prosecutor parading in front of the judge, asking questions and not letting people finish explaining. When Mr. Burke came forward, his face was pale and glum.

"I'm afraid so." He fidgeted, answering the prosecutor's questions without looking at Patrick's father. "I didn't believe it at first because he'd always appeared to be a good Christian man. But it appears John—the defendant—somehow became involved with the Fenians. I wish it weren't so."

Patrick's jaw dropped at Mr. Burke's testimony. He leaned over to whisper into his sister's ear, "He's lying! He's not standing up for Pa the way he said he would."

Becky frowned and shook her head, too. After all his promises of help, Mr. Burke was making it sound as if their father were some kind of criminal. No one was speaking up for the truth. *It can't be!* Patrick wanted to shout.

Next the angry prosecutor called the police inspector, the same one who caused all the trouble in the first place. The last witness, a wild-eyed character in a ragged shirt, also insisted that Patrick's father was a member of the Fenians.

"An outlaw—just like his father," concluded the prosecutor. "It is quite tragic that this man should follow in his father's footsteps as a lawbreaker."

Patrick felt his ears steaming at the man's words, even though he didn't understand them all. His parents had never told him anything about his father's father, their grandfather—only that he had left Ireland when their father was a young boy.

"What does he mean, Ma?" Michael complained in a loud whisper. "Why do they keep talking and talking? When are they going to let Pa come home with us?"

But by that time the judge looked as if he had heard enough.

"Oyez, oyez, oyez!" cried a small man in a dark uniform as the judge reentered the room after taking a short recess. "All manner of persons are commanded to keep silence whilst a sentence is passed upon the prisoner at the bar."

The judge looked over his glasses and sat down slowly. Patrick could not breathe, but he heard someone across the room cough quietly before the judge hammered his wooden gavel onto his desk for the last time.

"Guilty as charged."

No. Patrick closed his eyes and gritted his teeth as the judge's words echoed through the silent courtroom. *No!*

Frowning, the judge pulled a quill pen from an inkwell and scratched out his instructions on a piece of paper. "I understand this man has a family, but I regret there is no other alternative." He paused for a moment and rubbed his chin in thought.

Patrick's head spun.

"The prisoner shall spend the next ten years at hard labor in the prison colony of Western Australia. I've a good mind to seek restitution as well. You Fenians should pay back the government for the trouble you cause."

The prosecutor clapped his hands in victory.

Patrick's father squeezed his eyes shut and bowed his head slightly. It was too much for Patrick to watch.

"Pa!" he cried. Without thinking, he jumped from his seat and ran toward his father. The guard whirled around, but not fast enough.

"Patrick!" shouted his mother.

"Oh no, you don't, lad." The big guard stepped in front of his father and grabbed Patrick by the shoulders while the judge glanced up at the commotion with alarm.

"See here!" The judge dropped his pen and glared out at him. "We'll have none of this nonsense. Remove that boy immediately."

Patrick's father held out his hand, and Patrick could only touch his father's fingertips before he was yanked away and carried down the courtroom aisle to the outside door. A moment later he was deposited on the marble steps leading down to the street.

"You can't just drop him there," protested Becky. She had slipped through the crowd and followed them out.

But the guard only grunted and left Patrick and Becky alone on the steps. The sound of the tall iron doors slamming rang painfully in Patrick's ears.

"Becky, they can't!" He looked to his sister, but he knew she couldn't make anything better. She hadn't been able to make it better when Sean had drowned, though Patrick had looked to her then, too. Now she couldn't do anything when the police were taking away their father.

"Did you hear what the judge said?" she asked him, dusting off the knees of his best trousers. "Did you hear what he said about how Pa should pay a debt to society for his crime?"

"You mean the crime they *said* he did." Patrick sniffled and looked around. "It doesn't matter. We don't have any money to pay anyone."

Becky shook her head and grabbed her brother's hand. "Don't you understand? They took Pa away, and now they'll take everything we have!"

CHAPTER 4

THE NERVE OF THAT MAN

Becky was already down the steps and running across the street before Patrick finally understood what she had been talking about. The McWaids weren't rich, but with their father's good, steady job at the newspaper, they had a few nice things in their flat. Their mother's silver, even some family jewelry. It seemed impossible to think the police would take it, but then so had their father's arrest.

"You really think they're going to take our things?" Patrick flew through their front door after his sister.

"Don't you? I know where we can hide some."

Still breathing hard after the run home from the courthouse, Becky kneeled in a corner of their kitchen. Carefully, she lifted up a corner of the flooring, then slipped the things that Patrick brought her under the floorboards. A silver lampstand and a delicate glass vase. His mother's favorite music box.

"How about this?" asked Patrick, holding up their carved black mantel clock. His sister sighed.

"It's too big, Patrick. We can't hide everything."

He nodded and replaced the clock gently on the shelf above their coal parlor stove.

"Hurry up," urged Becky from the kitchen. "Someone could be coming!"

"I don't know . . ." Patrick hesitated at his parents' dresser. "I

31

feel strange going through Ma and Pa's belongings this way."

"You're not going through their things to be nosy," she reassured him. "We're just trying to save them from being taken."

Patrick held on to a small gold ring, a wedding band of some kind, with an unusual green stone.

"Is this Ma's?" he wondered aloud, but just then the front door clicked open.

"Patrick! Becky!" It was Michael. He came running into the kitchen as Becky hastily finished replacing the floorboards. "You're in trouble. They had to talk to Ma for a while, and she didn't know where you were."

"There you are." Their mother stood in the kitchen doorway, looking old and very tired. Her eyes were brimming with tears.

"Oh, Ma, I'm sorry." Becky ran into her mother's arms, and the two of them started to cry all over again. Patrick kept his hand around the ring in his pocket, wondering how to explain what they had been doing.

"I was worried about you two," she told them, giving Patrick a look and drying her tears. "You children are all I have now, and . . ."

"Ma, don't say that." But Patrick knew it was true.

"Please listen to me." She guided them to the kitchen table and sat down with a sigh. For a moment she held her head in her hands, then took a deep breath and looked up at them. "You heard them say they're sending your father to Australia."

All three children nodded, and their mother continued.

"We're going to try to follow him there."

There was a stunned silence for a long moment, then Becky crossed her arms.

"But it's not fair, Ma," she said. "We haven't done anything wrong."

"It just isn't fair!" agreed Patrick. "Pa hasn't done anything wrong, either. And now they're making us leave Dublin."

"I know that, children, and it makes me angry, too. But no one will believe your father or us. Goodness knows we've tried. No one believes anything your father said—not even his boss, it seems."

Patrick looked at his sister and brother and frowned.

"We'll just have to make a new life," their mother went on. "We'll be closer to your father in Australia."

"I don't like those people." Michael made a face and hid behind the folds of his mother's long, plain dress. "They were all mean liars."

"Do we have any money to get to Australia?" Becky twirled the edge of the white lace tablecloth between her fingers.

Mrs. McWaid shook her head. "A little, but not—"

A knock at the door interrupted her.

"Could you please answer that?" Their mother looked at Patrick, and he hesitated.

"I'll bet it's them!" he whispered to Becky, and she glanced over at the spot on the floor. The person at the door knocked again, louder.

"Patrick?" asked Mrs. McWaid.

Patrick took a deep breath, stood up, and shuffled to the door. When he cracked it open, he saw the dark black eyes of Conrad Burke. *Him again!*

"Ah, there you are, my boy," puffed Mr. Burke. He took out his handkerchief and blew his nose. "May I come in for just a moment?"

Patrick put his foot in front of the door to keep it from opening more than a couple of inches, then looked back at his mother. All their valuables were hidden, but . . .

"I just wanted to tell you how sorry I was at the outcome of the trial. The charges were an astonishing surprise to me as well . . . I was as saddened as you must be."

Patrick's mother appeared at Patrick's elbow, but she made no move to open the door wider.

"And, Mrs. McWaid, I just didn't want you to harbor any hard feelings. Perhaps I could even arrange to look in on John—"

"You don't need to," piped up Michael. "We're going ourselves."

Patrick turned to his brother with a finger in front of his lips.

"Oh, is that right?" Burke sounded interested. "Have you made arrangements?"

"Michael only meant that you needn't trouble yourself, sir," replied Mrs. McWaid. Patrick could almost feel the ice in her breath.

"I see. Well, I wanted to tell you that there's perhaps a possibility I could bring some influence to bear and arrange to have your husband released early. At least I could try."

Why is Burke saying all this? Patrick didn't understand what was going on or who this man really was.

"Yes, well." Mr. Burke replaced his hat on his head. "I just wanted you to know that I am truly sorry, and that I am not the villain I may appear to be."

"Good day to you, Mr. Burke." Patrick's mother never uncrossed her arms.

Burke finally backed away from the door, and Patrick pushed it shut with a sigh of relief.

"The nerve of that man," began their mother.

"After all the lies he said about Pa during the trial," agreed Michael. He puffed out his chest and imitated Mr. Burke. "What an astonishing surprise!"

"At least he didn't get our things." Becky stepped over to their hiding place and pulled up the floorboards. "Patrick and I hid them under the floor, Ma."

At first their mother didn't understand. "What things are you talking about?"

When Becky and Patrick showed her, their mother smiled for the first time in a month.

"See, Ma?" Patrick held up a shining silver plate. "Becky said they were going to come and take all our things away to pay for Pa's crime."

Mrs. McWaid shook her head. "I know what the judge said. But no one's going to take our things."

Becky wasn't sure. "They said Pa had to pay for his crimes, and I just thought—"

"First of all, your father has no crime to pay for. And second of all, no one is coming for our things." She held one of her silver candlesticks and rubbed the shine absently. "But you children just gave me an idea. Becky, pull everything out of there and put it in a pillowcase. We're going to the pawnbrokers."

"But, Ma," protested Patrick. This time he knew exactly what his mother was saying. "You can't."

"I can and I will. Candlesticks and silver plates do us no good if we can't be together as a family. With passage to Australia, at least we'll be on the same continent as your father. Surely the pawnbrokers will give us enough to pay our way."

CHAPTER 5

MEMORIES FOR SALE

Patrick Street. Where the poorest of Dublin brought second-hand clothes, dishes, and even their beds to pawn.

"It's almost like selling the things, Michael," Becky explained as they threaded their way through the crowds. She and her mother each carried a bulging pillowcase of their family's prized possessions. "People who need money bring their things to the pawnbrokers."

"People like us," said Michael. His mother frowned but said nothing.

"Then they can buy it back later," added Patrick. "Usually after Saturday payday, when they have more money."

"A lot more money," said Mrs. McWaid. "Pawnbrokers sell for more than they buy. And they don't buy for very much."

"But how do we buy the stuff back if we're in Australia, Ma?" Michael wanted to know.

"We don't." Mrs. McWaid pushed open the door to a small, dark shop. Patrick could hardly read the faded lettering on the window: *E. Donegal, Pawnbroker.*

"Hello?" Mrs. McWaid looked into the store, cautiously holding Becky back with her right arm while Michael slipped by. Mr. E. Donegal, if that's who it was, had one of just about everything in his crowded, stuffy shop. A violin propped up next to a mismatched set of pewter mugs and a pile of chipped china plates. An old portrait of a prince in a gaudy gold frame. Patrick sneezed twice from the damp, musty smell that seemed to come from everything. Michael quickly discovered a ruffled green-and-red parrot sitting on a perch in a corner.

"Off with their heads!" squawked the parrot, and Michael laughed.

"Oh!" Patrick jumped. "I thought it was stuffed."

"Mind the bird" came a voice from the darkness in the back of the store, "or he'll take your ear off."

Michael gave the bird a respectable distance but still stared. "You think he says anything else?" he wondered aloud.

"Oh, to be sure." A mouse of a man crawled up on a chair behind a dusty glass counter and surveyed them through thick glasses. The deep voice should have belonged to someone else, and Patrick wanted to look behind the counter to see if a puppeteer was hiding.

"I'm not buying any more old clothes today," announced the man.

Surely he can see we aren't carrying clothes, Patrick thought.

"No clothes." Mrs. McWaid laid her pillowcase carefully on the counter.

"Ah, so I see." The tiny man's glasses magnified his eyeballs, and he felt on the counter a couple of times before he made contact with the pillowcase.

Can he see? wondered Patrick.

In the corner, Michael was trying to get the parrot to say something else.

"I'm late!" shouted the man, picking up a candlestick and holding it so close to his face, Patrick thought he was going to eat it. The man's words made no sense.

"I'm late!" repeated the parrot. "I'm late!"

Michael laughed again. "From *Alice in Wonderland*. Does he say anything else?"

"Michael, stay away from that bird," warned Mrs. McWaid. She looked worriedly from her son to the little man sampling her candlestick.

"No harm done, madam." E. Donegal swiveled one eye up at her like a lizard. Patrick shivered and took a step backward as the man ran a wiry finger along the edge of a silver spoon and smiled.

"Pity." The gnome of a man mumbled something else that Patrick couldn't make out, then went back to rummaging through their pillowcases.

"Poor Alice," echoed the bird.

Patrick had started to look at a dusty stack of books on Christopher Columbus and Ferdinand Magellan, but the moldy smell made his stomach feel queasy. He made a face.

"You're so sweet." The parrot ruffled its feathers.

"Why don't you get some fresh air, Patrick?" his mother suggested. Patrick nodded.

"Pity," Patrick heard the pawnbroker mumble again. "Of course it's worth more, but for a fact, no one on Patrick Street will give you more than Evan Donegal—"

The door shut behind him with a jingle of bells.

Patrick breathed easier outside, and the early September sunshine felt good. Through the grimy window, he could barely see Mr. Donegal showing his mother and Becky some figures on a pad. The bird screeched. Finally Mrs. McWaid looked down and nodded weakly, then peeled the couple of coins that the pawnbroker had shoved in her direcon off the counter. Patrick took a step backward as Becky came flying out of the store.

"Ma!" His sister sounded upset. "How could you let him steal our things?"

"Michael, come along now!" Mrs. McWaid ignored the question as she paused for a moment at the door. Michael shuffled out of the store with a final look back. Patrick could see the pawnbroker grinning over his pile of loot.

"Ma, can I come back sometime and see if I can get the parrot to say something else? All he says are things from *Alice in Wonderland*."

"Off with her head!" screeched the bird as Mrs. McWaid let the door slam behind her.

Patrick's mother stooped down on the sidewalk and looked Michael straight in the eye.

"Michael, you are never to come near this place again, do you hear me?"

Michael looked confused. "But, Ma—"

"But nothing." She stood up and marched them all down the street in the direction of home. "Between now and the time we leave for Australia, you and your brother are not to even come this direction."

Patrick glanced back at the sooty window. He didn't want to come back.

"Patrick, how much money do we need to get to Australia?" Michael asked as they followed their mother home.

Patrick was halfheartedly searching for pennies and halfpennies between the cobblestones. "More than what Mr. Donegal gave us."

"A lot more?"

Patrick looked up at his sister, who returned his half smile.

"A lot more, Michael."

"We could put the zebras over here, away from the lions." Michael concentrated on the zoo drawing on his slate as the others prepared for dinner several days later. Patrick smiled at his brother as he helped his mother peel potatoes.

"Ma, could we sell this?" Michael held up the drawing he had just made.

"No, Michael," she told him gently. "It's too good to sell."

"Really?" Michael beamed and changed the subject as only he could do. "Patrick said we should find another pawnbroker for the ring."

His mother gave Patrick a quick look. Grandmother's ring was still hanging on a string around his neck, and Patrick wasn't sure why she had let him keep it.

"No," she finally said. " 'Twas a good thought, but no. There's no value to selling all our memories."

"Why not, Ma?" Michael quizzed his mother. "We sold all our other things already, and we still don't have enough money to get to Australia, do we?"

"I wish I could do something," offered Becky, putting out the four forks and knives they hadn't yet sold. "And I wonder how they're treating Pa. I miss him."

Mrs. McWaid scalped a potato savagely as Becky set the rest of the table. Patrick could see her tears falling as the potato whittled down to almost nothing.

"We all miss your father," she whispered. "But I've had to use what little money we gained to buy food. There's not enough, and there are no jobs. I'm sorry. . . ."

"But, Ma, we've prayed," said Michael, not looking up from his drawing. "God is going to help us find a way to go with Pa."

Becky stopped with a dish in her hands. Mrs. McWaid straightened up, smiled, and put down her knife.

"Out of the mouths of babes."

"I'm not a babe, Ma," protested Michael.

Their mother laughed. "Just an expression, child."

"A Bible verse," added Becky.

"Well, yes. One of your father's favorite verses, in fact. It's just that the youngest sometimes say the best things."

"But not always," put in Patrick.

Michael made a face at his older brother. "But what did I say?"

Mrs. McWaid reached over and patted Michael on the cheek. Becky pulled Patrick aside and whispered into his ear. "I've an idea how we can get to Australia."

"How?" Patrick whispered back. He wasn't sure why they were whispering.

Becky only shook her head. "I can't tell you now. Tomorrow. But I'm going to need your help."

CHAPTER 6

A SECRET FRIEND

The next afternoon Patrick shivered despite the warm sun and looked nervously up and down the busy street.

"I don't know about this, Becky."

"If you don't want to do this, you can go home."

"That's not what I mean."

"Well?" Becky leaned against the corner of O'Reilly's Shoe Store, Limited, where the latest fashions for women were displayed in the windows.

Patrick shaded his eyes and peered up at the steps of the courthouse. "What if he won't stop?" he wanted to know.

"Maybe he won't." Becky set her jaw. "But no one else can help us."

"All right. So when the judge steps out of the courthouse, I run straight at him and—"

"And I'll go for the carriage."

The bells at nearby St. Michan's Church rang four o'clock, then five, and still no carriage arrived for the Honorable Judge Harold S. Dalrymple. The same judge who had pounded the gavel down in the courtroom when Patrick and Becky's father had been convicted.

"He doesn't *live* in there, does he?" Patrick hopped up and down on one foot. "Ma's going to start wondering where we are."

"Look!" Becky nudged her brother. They both noticed the black horse-drawn carriage, finer than most. It was driven by a black-suited groom who stared straight ahead and pulled the team up short at the foot of the steps.

"He's going to come rushing down those steps in a minute." Becky straightened her dress.

"How do you know?"

"That's what he did every day of the trial, remember?" She didn't take her eyes off the tall iron doors. "About four or five o'clock, he pulled his pocket watch from his vest and then left. Every day, the same thing."

As she spoke, the doors flew open and a tall, gray-haired man stepped into the afternoon sunshine, adjusted his collar, and headed for the carriage. He looked different without his white starched wig, but it had to be the judge.

"Now!" Becky whispered to her brother. They both lunged forward.

"Your Honor, sir!" cried Patrick as the man came down the stairs. Like a newspaper reporter running for a story, Patrick took a couple of steps up to meet him, and a man walking just behind the judge stepped out in front.

"Out of the way, urchin!" warned the guard, as if he would sweep Patrick aside with the back of his enormous, hairy hand.

"I'm not a beggar," Patrick said, ducking lower. "I just want to ask the judge about my father."

"I said be gone!" The guard would have picked Patrick up by the back of the shirt if the judge had not stopped him.

"No, wait," the judge spoke up in his fine London accent. He put his hands on his knees and looked Patrick straight in the eyes. "Who's your father, boy? Someone in my court?"

"Yes, Your Honor." Patrick nodded.

"And where do you live?"

"Thirty-three Swifts Alley, sir," Patrick replied.

"Please, Your Honor," Becky spoke up from behind Patrick, and the judge straightened up.

"Oh, so it's the two of you," he said. "Now I remember. You're the children of that McWaid fellow. So why are you assaulting me here on the courthouse steps?"

"We must go with him to Australia, sir," Becky blurted. "Can't you let us sail on the same ship with him? Is there not a way?"

The judge narrowed his eyes. "That's not done anymore. You don't have the fare for your own passage, I gather?"

Patrick could only stare at the cobblestone street.

"No, Your Honor," he heard his sister answer. "We've sold most of our valuables for food. Our mother's trying her best to keep the family together."

"Come, Becky." Patrick tugged at the sleeve of his sister's blouse. "We shouldn't have bothered him."

"No, wait." The man's voice sounded less harsh. "I . . . ah, believe I can sympathize with your situation."

Becky looked up shyly. "You can?"

The judge rubbed his forehead nervously and rocked back on his heels. "I lost my own father at an early age. So, yes, I can understand . . . perhaps."

His voice trailed away, and he looked above them, seemingly lost in thought.

"Sir," interrupted the guard, still looking perturbed, "the earl is expecting you. We must be leaving."

"Yes, yes, of course." Judge Dalrymple woke from his daydream. "I'm sorry to hear of your difficulties, but I'm afraid there's nothing I can do to help you at this point. Your father, well, he was just following after what his father did, was he not?"

"I don't know, Your Honor." Patrick shook his head and turned away.

"It was a good try, Patrick," whispered his sister, coming up beside him. But Becky wasn't any more cheerful than he felt. They threaded their way home through the early evening crowds.

"Why do they keep mentioning our grandfather?" Patrick wondered aloud.

Becky sighed. "I don't know. When I asked Ma, she just started crying again. She promised to tell me later."

"She never talks to me about Pa's family. All she's ever said to me about our grandfather is that he went away to Australia when Pa was a boy."

His sister shrugged as she reached for the door to their flat. "Patrick, who went away to Australia back then besides prisoners?"

"But didn't he ever write? Didn't Pa try to write him? Would he not—"

"I don't know. Ma told me once that they heard he went to a place called Echuca, but he never answered their letters."

"Why wouldn't he?"

Becky shrugged. "That's what we don't know."

"Funny name," Patrick said as they slipped into the kitchen. "Eh-choo—"

"Bless you," said their mother. "Get washed up for supper."

"Where have you been?" chirped Michael from his spot on the floor. "You two went without me."

"Sorry, Michael." Becky smiled at her little brother. "Patrick and I were just—" She stopped in midsentence at the concerned look on her mother's face.

"Yes?" asked Mrs. McWaid, raising an eyebrow.

"We went to see the judge," squeaked Patrick.

"You did what?" Mrs. McWaid's eyes grew big.

"Becky thought that if we waited for the judge, we might be able to talk him into letting us sail on the same ship as Pa."

Their mother clapped her hands. "Mercy! Next you'll be breaking windows so as to be arrested and transported to Australia yourselves."

"That's a pretty good idea, Ma." Becky dared a grin. "We should have thought of that."

"You already know that wouldn't work." Mrs. McWaid chuckled for a moment, then caught herself and was dead serious once more. "The judge said that your father may be the last prisoner sent to Australia. The Australians don't want prisoners anymore."

"If they don't want him," said Becky, "we'll keep him."

"It's still not fair." Patrick sighed and leaned his head against the wall. "We can't even visit him."

"And we've no money to pay our own way to Australia besides," Becky added the obvious.

There was nothing left to say, so they washed for supper in the kitchen washbasin. Even Michael was silent, so when something rustled under the door, they all turned at once.

"What's that?" Patrick stepped over to pick up a small, flat bundle wrapped in heavy brown paper. His mother took it from him with a puzzled expression while he checked the shadowy hallway. No one.

"No address." Mrs. McWaid carefully tore the paper away from the bundle—and froze.

"Ma?" Becky leaned over her plate to see, and her mouth fell open as well when she saw what was inside the envelope. Her mother emptied a small pile of gold coins onto the middle of the table, where they rolled all over.

" 'See to it that this money is applied only to your fare and expenses to Australia,' " Patrick read the small, careful script on the note. " 'This should be enough to keep your family together, after a fashion. God be with you.' "

"Who?" stuttered their mother, but the instructions were unsigned. "Surely not that Burke fellow again."

"It wasn't Burke." Patrick dropped the note and jumped up to look out their only window, a small opening to the crowded street outside. "He wouldn't say 'God be with you.' And he wouldn't help us."

Outside, a stout wagon loaded high with barrels lumbered past the door, the driver urging his team on. There were others, too: a small two-wheeled cart pulled by a single horse; and a handsome black cab, like the judge's, disappearing around the corner to Francis Street.

Michael whooped and jumped. "We're rich!" he cried. "And now we can go! I knew God would give us the money. I just knew it."

"Ma," Becky laughed. "He's right."

By that time Patrick and his brother were dancing in circles, skipping around the kitchen. Patrick knew the money wouldn't make them rich, but it *was* enough for fare to Australia.

"It was Judge Dalrymple," said Becky, also looking out the window. "It had to be."

"Why would he do that?" wondered their mother, still looking dazed.

Patrick wasn't sure, but he knew one thing: Before it was too late, he had to visit his father in prison. *Someone has to tell him we're going to Australia, too.* This time, Patrick decided, he would do it alone.

CHAPTER 7

LAST GOOD-BYE

"Stop shaking, Patrick," Patrick whispered to himself as he stepped toward the tall, castlelike Kilmainham Jail. "All they can say is no again, the way they did to Ma."

A guard in front frowned when Patrick explained what he wanted, but he stepped aside and opened one of the tall black-iron doors placed into the thick, rough granite. Patrick shivered as he stepped into a guardhouse. A high counter stood in front of him. Beyond that was another set of double doors and the massive prison.

"Father in heaven," he whispered in a soft prayer, "all I ask is one time with Pa. I just have to tell him."

"What? Speak up?" came a scratchy, unsteady voice from behind the counter.

Patrick opened his eyes to see a jailkeeper leaning back in his chair. The middle-aged man had sharp yellow teeth and a week's stubble of beard. He caught his balance and stared at Patrick over a desk strewn with assorted keys, chains, and faded newspapers.

"Talking to yerself?" asked the man.

"No, sir." Patrick gulped. "I just came to visit my pa."

The man spit in the direction of a bucket on the floor, wiped his mouth on the sleeve of a frayed black coat, and inspected Patrick with bloodshot eyes. He looked around the empty room, grunted, and put on a sickly, pretend grin.

"Ah, you just came to visit your pa, did you?" he mimicked Patrick's voice. "Don't that just warrum the cockles of me heart." The man spat once more and rummaged through his desktop collection, mumbling something about caretaking for street urchins while everyone else was eating lunch. He eventually came up with a half-gnawed chicken leg and, brushing away a fly, took a big bite. "You hungry, lad?"

Patrick shook his head. *Not anymore.*

The man shrugged and seemed in no hurry as he casually waved Patrick behind the counter. "Come on, then, who'll you be here to see?"

Patrick couldn't believe it was going to be so easy. "McWaid. My father's name is John McWaid."

The jailer paused in his chewing and looked carefully down at Patrick. "So it is. D'you know, boy, we've strict orders not to allow visitors for that one." He gave a satisfied burp. "Of course, when I'm left in charge, we work by my rules. Come on, lad."

Patrick was afraid to say anything else, but he followed the man through a pair of heavy doors, past several guards, and down a dark hall lined with rusty iron bars and grim little cells. He shivered. Everything everywhere seemed coated in a horrible, dripping smell that clung like a dark cloud to the damp, mossy walls.

They walked past what seemed like caves full of men, many dressed in rags, hiding in the shadows. Once, Patrick nearly stepped on a black shape that scurried and squealed between him and the jailer.

"A cat!" he cried.

The jailer replied without turning around, "'Ere's no cats in this jail. Every time we bring one in, the rats carry 'im off."

Patrick heard his footsteps echo on the cold wood-planked floor, and he tried not to look inside the cells as he passed by. But the hollow eyes followed him, and he could not stop shivering, could not shake the unpleasant feeling of being watched.

"'E's not in there, if that's what you're wondering," said the jailer, running his keys across the bars with a clattering noise. Finally they entered a hall-like auditorium, three stories high and topped by an enormous set of skylights. Three levels of balconies lined the walls, each with dozens of doors. A long staircase in the middle of the floor led up to the second level.

"Quit gawking, lad. You want to see your pa or not?"

Patrick followed along as close as he dared while the man shouted at some of the prisoners like a circus performer shouted at a lion in a cage.

"You work in this place too long, lad, and you either learn to deal with it, as I have, or you go bats."

After they climbed the staircase to the second level, Patrick looked up at one of the small windows in the doors to see a pair of dark, hollow eyes staring back. He shivered and got into step with the jailer. The auditorium seemed endless and filled with cries. Somewhere in the distance he could hear a guard barking orders.

"How much farther?" asked Patrick.

The jailer ignored his question. "Does your ma know you're here, or is she behind bars, too?"

Patrick bit his lip. "She doesn't know. And she's certainly not—"

"I thought as much."

The man slowed and started counting numbers on the cell doors. "Eighteen, let me see . . . Eighteen, you're still in there?"

There was a growl from behind one of the doors from Mr. Eighteen, whoever he was. Satisfied, the jailer kept walking down the hallway until they came to door twenty-nine. He stopped and kicked at it with his heavy boot. "All right, McWaid, you've a visitor."

Patrick's heart beat faster at the mention of his last name. Behind that door . . .

There was a shuffling, and a face appeared at the tiny window.

"Pa?" Patrick stood on his tiptoes to see through the iron bars. He was nose to nose with a man he hardly recognized. Two months in jail had hollowed out his father's cheeks, pulled his eyes back into his head, and given him an ashy complexion. The man stood shivering with a threadbare blanket wrapped around his shoulders. But it *was* Pa!

For a minute they only stared at each other, Patrick too astonished at the way his father looked to think of anything to say. After a long moment, a new twinkle seemed to light up his father's face.

"How did you get in here, son?" His voice was soft and hoarse. He looked quickly past Patrick's face to see who had brought him in. "O'Brien, can you open the door for a moment?"

The jailer laughed but kept his arms crossed on his chest. "I may be crazy, but I'm no fool." O'Brien looked around nervously. "Or maybe I am, allowing this urchin in here. Say what you have to say before someone sees I'm gone from the front desk."

"Are you all right, Pa?" Patrick was sorry for the words as soon as they were out. *Of course he's not all right,* he told himself. *Not in this stinking prison.*

His father smiled and nodded. "I'll be fine, son. And you're a wonderful sight. How about your ma?"

"She's all right. Becky and Michael are fine, too."

"Good, good . . ." Mr. McWaid's voice trailed off, and then they heard a high-pitched wail from down the hall.

"Ahh, Eighteen, quit yer complaining!" bellowed the guard, shuffling away to investigate. He pulled out a well-worn billy club from his belt and pointed it at Patrick. "You stay there. I'll be right back."

"He won't go anywhere," promised Patrick's father.

"Pa, tell me about your father. Grandfather." Patrick surprised even himself when he blurted it out. He hadn't been thinking about his grandfather, only about seeing Pa.

Mr. McWaid seemed just as surprised as he. "Is that what you came here to ask me?" The question was gentle, the twinkle still there.

Patrick shook his head in embarrassment.

"Uh, no, not exactly. I don't know why I said that. You don't—"

Down the hall the guard banged against Mr. Eighteen's cell door with his club.

"That's all right," continued Patrick's father. "I could tell during the trial that you were surprised to hear your grandfather mentioned. But I might as well tell you."

For just a brief moment Patrick imagined himself on his father's knee as a child, looking into Pa's eyes as he told stories of a magic koala bear somewhere in the eucalyptus woods of the new frontier of Australia. Stories of giant hopping creatures called kangaroos. It seemed so long ago, but here was the same pair of eyes and his father about to tell him a story—this one all too true.

"I'm sorry we never told you, son." Patrick's father barely managed to choke out the words. "We thought we were protecting you and your sister."

"Protecting us from what?"

His father cleared his throat and coughed. "From knowing your grandfather was some kind of criminal. . . ."

"What did he do?" whispered Patrick.

"Stole a sheep. It was during the famine, you see. That doesn't make it right, but he was desperate for food. So they sent him to jail—this jail—and then off to Australia."

"I still don't understand." Patrick had almost forgotten about the jailer, who was just returning down the hallway. "Why did he not write to you? Or did he?"

Patrick's father shook his head sadly. "After he left, my mother—your grandmother—died of tuberculosis. I think something broke inside of him when he heard what happened. And I don't think he knew the Lord. At least he never told me about God."

He paused again, obviously wrestling with his painful memory. "I was about your age. Spent the rest of my school days with an uncle and aunt. I don't know where they sent my two brothers."

"But didn't you try to write your pa?"

"Goodness, yes. Many times. All I got back was a reply from a prison official, saying that my father had been released, didn't want contact with anyone, and was last heard from in a town on the Murray River called Echuca."

"Echuca. That's what Becky said."

The jailer, who had returned, stomped his foot for attention. "This is all very lovely, but—"

Mr. McWaid held up his hand. "Just another minute. Please?"

The jailer frowned but took a step back and kept silent. At the same instant they saw someone across the auditorium, pointing at them.

"O'Brien!" that someone called out. "What's going on over there?"

The jailer jerked Patrick away from the door.

"That's it, boy," he hissed, dragging Patrick by the arm. "I'm in trouble. Back out the way we came!"

Patrick tried to reach through the little window in the door, but he was too far away.

"Wait!" Patrick tried to drag his feet. "I didn't get a chance to—"

O'Brien clamped a hand over his mouth.

"Quiet!" he hissed, pulling Patrick away.

The last thing Patrick saw of his father was a hand pressed through the bars in the door, reaching toward him.

"You know the truth, Patrick," his father reassured him. "Don't forget the truth!"

"We're going to follow you, Pa!" Patrick tried to yell, but he couldn't get the words out. The jailer kept a hand on his mouth to silence him until they were far enough down the hall.

"What was I thinking, letting you go back there?" the jailer grumbled sourly, nearly pulling Patrick's arm from its socket as they hurried down the stairway ahead of the other voice.

"I saw you there, O'Brien," called a man, but the jailer didn't respond.

"What about tomorrow?" Patrick wondered aloud. "If I brought my ma back here around the same time, could we—"

"No," interrupted the man, by then flushed and sweating, "not a chance in the world. If Mr. Burke hears that I—" He caught himself as they hurried past the large cells full of prisoners, then burst past the guards and into the front entry hall.

"So it's true," said Patrick, breathing hard. "Burke and his friends made sure that Pa was put in prison. Now he's making sure Pa doesn't talk to anyone while he's here. Isn't that it?"

Patrick blinked and held a hand in front of his eyes at the sunshine that streamed in the front windows.

"Better shut your mouth if you know what's good for you."

"Just tell me it's true." Patrick was guessing, but it was growing clear that Burke was more than just his father's boss at the newspaper. Much more.

"Nothing's true, boy, and don't ever let me see you around here again."

Patrick tried to turn around, but he felt himself pushed through the front door. He fell to his knees in the street, the sound of the slamming metal door ringing in his ears.

"Thanks for letting me see Pa," he whispered to no one, kicking a pebble as hard as he could. "But I didn't get to tell him what I came for."

"Hello there, boy," called someone from the street. "Most people are happy to walk out of that place."

Patrick glanced up to see a cab driver looking down at him from his perch at the front of a carriage. His single white horse held up its hooves nervously until Patrick scrambled to his feet and hurried out of the cab's way.

"I know you told me the jailer pushed you out yesterday, Patrick." Becky prodded her brother down the street, around a couple of parked wagons. "But it's worth another try anyway, don't you think?"

Patrick sighed. "Of course it's worth a try. I want to see Pa again as much as you."

"I know. But I wouldn't want to meet up with that crazy jailer, either."

Patrick sighed with relief a minute later when they didn't see O'Brien behind the counter. An older man sat in his place, sorting through a pile of papers. He didn't look up, so Becky cleared her throat.

"Excuse me, sir," she tried. "We're here to see our father, if it might be allowed."

The man kept his finger in the pile of papers and looked up with a trace of a cruel, bored grin.

"McWaid?" Becky squeaked.

The man shook his head. "You can't see him."

"But I saw him yesterday." Patrick didn't want to get the jailer who had helped him in trouble, but he was ready to try anything. "A man named O'Brien let me see him."

The older fellow raised his silver eyebrows. "As of yesterday, O'Brien doesn't work here anymore. A wild, no-good waster with a whiskey nose on him before he was in trousers, if you ask me. He knew better than to take you back there."

"So you're saying we can't see our father?" Becky asked more boldly.

The man made no attempt to cover a yawn. "Couldn't if I wanted to, miss. He's been taken to London this morning. Now, get along."

"London?" Patrick couldn't believe it.

"You know the city. Last stop before they're on to beautiful Australia."

Patrick didn't like the way the man sneered at them, so he tugged at his sister's sleeve. "It's no use, Becky. Let's go."

"No, wait." Becky still wasn't satisfied. "Could you tell me when our father is scheduled to leave England?" she asked him sweetly.

"If you promise to leave me alone." The man sighed and thumbed through his papers. Becky smiled and held Patrick's hand hard so he wouldn't leave. The man glanced up again, looking more exasperated than ever.

"He's leaving on the *Hougoumont* with 278 other Fenians and criminals in one week." He pronounced the name *WHO-go-mont*. "They should arrive in about three months at the prison colony in Western Australia, sometime in January. Now, if you don't mind . . ."

"Thank you so much." Becky let go of Patrick's hand and slipped out backward through the door.

Outside the building, Patrick leaned against the brick and tried to imagine where his father was just then. Shackled in the back of a wagon, maybe, or in the hold of a rotten prison ship. He wasn't sure.

"It doesn't matter, Patrick," his sister tried to encourage him. "God is going to take us to Pa. I know He is. When Ma finds a ship for us, we'll be on our way."

CHAPTER 8

DUBLIN DISAPPEARS

"Patrick, wake up."

Patrick's eyes seemed glued shut, but he managed to pry them open the third time his sister shook him by the shoulders.

"Ma and Michael are already awake," Becky whispered in his ear. "We're leaving."

That was all he needed to hear. It had been two and a half months since the money was slipped under their door, the longest ten weeks of Patrick's life. Christmas had come and gone as if it were just another winter day, then New Year's Day, with no gifts and little cheer. No one had been able to celebrate—not Patrick or Becky. Not their mother. Not even Michael could celebrate without their father. The only thing that mattered was getting on a ship to Australia.

Maybe we'll be able to celebrate then, Patrick thought, peeking out the window at the street. The big day had finally arrived—January 5, 1868—and a carriage stood waiting in the cold morning air to take them to the pier.

"How far is it?" asked Michael once they were sitting in the crowded covered carriage. Patrick held on for balance.

"A half-hour drive, maybe," Patrick guessed, trying to remember what his mother had told the driver. "Down North Strand Road to the Vitriol Works and then along the Wharf Road."

"That's where we'll see the fishing boats." Michael tried to see out the window and past the high stone walls. "Remember when we saw them last summer?"

Patrick nodded. Eventually, they could make out the swinging cranes and the jumble of masts, shouting drivers, and groaning carts.

"Waterfront," shouted the driver almost before they had stopped.

"It's so big!" Michael stood for a moment on the dock and leaned his head back to take in the three tall masts.

Patrick nodded. It was true. Up close, the white-hulled *Star of Africa* was too big to look at all at once. Everywhere on deck, sailors were busy checking the spider's web of ropes that led upward. A few stretched between the three or four poles that hung sideways across each mast, as if they were crossing a T.

"Why are they up there on those poles, Ma?" asked Michael, still staring.

"Yardarms," a young sailor stepped up and corrected him.

"What?" Michael looked at him strangely.

"Yardarms," repeated the sailor. He looked about sixteen, with big, calloused hands and arms that almost burst through the sleeves of his blue woolen sweater. And he spoke with a strange accent, not the way Patrick assumed everyone on an English ship would speak. "They're called yardarms, and I think you'll learn a lot more sailor talk before this trip is through. May I take some of your bags?"

Mrs. McWaid smiled at the help and stepped carefully up the short plank that served as a way aboard the *Star of Africa*. The young sailor hoisted a couple of bags as if they were toys. Michael followed close behind, but Patrick and his sister hung back.

"I'm Michael McWaid." Patrick's little brother happily piled his bag on top of their mother's. "We're from Dublin. You don't talk like any person I've ever heard."

The young sailor laughed and adjusted his load. "Jefferson Pitney, pleased to meet you. I'm American—from the South, which may explain why you think I talk oddly. Arkansas. Just about everyone else aboard this ship is Scottish or English."

Mrs. McWaid looked around expectantly. "Any other passengers?"

"You're the only ones this trip—that's what Captain Smithgall says. Mostly we haul cargo. Follow me, and I'll show you where you'll be staying." He caught Michael's eye with a wink. "I'll show you the captain's bear, too."

Patrick grinned as Michael's eyes grew wide.

"You mean it?" his brother asked.

"Come see." The young sailor turned toward the ship's main cabin with his load of heavy bags. Patrick looked uncertainly down at the dark green water sloshing between the pretty white hull of the ship and the dock. Suddenly his throat turned dry, his hands sweaty.

There's nothing to be afraid of, he told himself. *This is not where Sean drowned. This is different*.

If it *was* different, Patrick couldn't convince his feet of it, and he wasn't able to move another step closer to the water.

Only Becky seemed to know what was happening. "It's going to be okay," she whispered to him. Michael and their mother had already disappeared into the ship. "This looks as if it's a really nice ship."

Patrick nodded and tried to will his feet to move, but they would not. Instead, he closed his eyes and gripped the handle of his big suitcase as if it were a lifeline.

"You can't stay here on the dock while we go to see Pa in Australia, little brother." Becky kept her voice down so no one else could hear them, but none of the sailors or dock workers paid them any attention.

"I know. I just didn't know it was going to be like this."

Patrick took a deep breath and tried to flush the sight of the water from his mind. The seawater stared him in the face like the river that had swallowed up Sean, daring him to get closer.

"We may not get wet the whole trip," continued Becky. "Remember how the man who sold us the tickets said these ships travel to Australia for wool and coal all the time? It takes them just three months now. Only three months until we're there. Then we'll be together as a family again."

"Only after Pa gets out of prison. It'll be years yet."

"God's taking care of him. Something good will happen. You'll see."

Patrick couldn't bring himself to open his eyes while Becky took his arm and gently pulled him toward the ship.

Lord, there's nothing to be afraid of, is there? This is all very silly. He finally pried his feet from the safety of the dock and shuffled up the swaying gangplank ahead of Becky. The ship's teakwood deck seemed solid enough, though it swayed gently in the Dublin Harbor tide.

"See?" whispered Becky as Michael launched out of a set of double doors that led from the main cabin.

"He was right!" Michael bubbled and grabbed them both by the arm. "There's really a bear down there."

"A stuffed bear, you mean." Becky almost stumbled. "Someone's leftover Christmas present, probably."

Michael shook his head energetically and hopped up and down. "You have to see."

Patrick thought he heard a growling squeal, and his mother hurried up out of the main cabin, her face pale.

"Ma, is there really a bear down there?" asked Becky.

Her mother nodded. "You stay away from that beast. No telling what it might do."

"But he's a pet, Ma," Michael said. "Let me show them, please?"

"He's quite tame, Mrs. McWaid, I assure you. Just a small Asian sun bear." A gray-bearded man in a blue suit jacket stepped up and bowed slightly to Patrick's mother. Judging by the gold braid on the bill of his cap, there was no doubt he was the captain. "It is Mrs. McWaid, correct?"

"Yes, I'm Sarah McWaid." She introduced the children in turn before the captain was called away by one of the sailors.

"Just be careful around suppertime." He looked back over his shoulder and winked at Michael. "The little rascal gets hungry, and he may be prone to sample your fingers as soon as his meal."

Suppertime, the captain had said. Patrick's stomach rumbled at the word. After the past few weeks of thin onion soup and wondering about the next meal, meals aboard the ship would seem like feasts. Their mother had done her best to earn extra money to pay the rent until they could get on a ship. Without Pa around, though, he knew it had not been easy.

"Show us the bear," Patrick commanded Michael before their mother could say anything else. For a moment he forgot about his fear of the water as they followed Michael four steps down a short stair ladder and into the ship's main salon. About the size of a small living room, it was furnished in rich wood furniture, a dining table with a little railing around the edge, upholstered chairs, blue glass kerosene lamps, and even a small collection of books on a wall shelf. Patrick thought it would be a wonderful room to explore later in the voyage. But right now the American sailor was shouting in the hallway ahead.

"Get off me, Ebony! Down!"

Another growl, and in a moment Patrick could see Jefferson Pitney standing on his tiptoes, holding a piece of moldy bread in the air. Climbing his leg was a furry bear cub with a light stripe across his chest, looking very much like a lively stuffed toy. The bear's glassy black eyes were focused on the treat, and his long pink tongue dangled from his muzzle. If the cub sat down, Patrick guessed he would probably not stand much taller than Jefferson's knees.

"Can we feed him?" Michael wanted to know.

"Sure, he'll eat about anything. Just watch out for his teeth." Jefferson tossed the bread to Michael, and the cub followed his prize over to the much smaller boy.

In a moment Michael was rolling on the floor, giggling and surrendering the bread.

"Michael!" Becky lunged forward to pick up her brother, but Jefferson only laughed.

"It's all right. Ebony is Captain Smithgall's new pet. Picked him up back in Borneo, hardly alive. The cook fed him fish soup from a bottle all the way over. He's just now started to eat lots of different things."

Patrick caught himself laughing at the sight of his brother on the floor of the salon, feeding bread to a bear. Above them on the deck, they could hear sailors scurrying back and forth, and officers shouting commands as they made ready to leave Dublin's harbor in the bitter cold breeze.

"Pitney!" Another sailor shouted down from the deck. "Are you finished with the passengers? We need you on the mooring lines. Time to shove off."

"Yes, sir—all except for their father." Jefferson looked over at Becky, who was helping Michael to his feet. "Isn't he coming?"

Becky turned red and stuttered for a moment, then quickly recovered. "He went ahead on another ship. We're supposed to meet him in Australia."

"Oh." Jefferson looked puzzled, but he spread out his arms. "Well, then, welcome to the *Star of Africa*. Your floating home for the next eighty-five days, or maybe less if we run into fair winds on our way to the other side of the world."

"Where's our room?" wondered Michael. "Do we get windows?"

Jefferson laughed. "No windows. You have two cabins just down this hallway and below. Usually, they're for junior officers, so each has two bunks and a little wash bowl. Better than the foc'sl, anyway."

"Folk-what?" asked Michael. Patrick had never heard the word, either.

"Folk-sull." The sailor pronounced it carefully. "The front of the ship where the sailors sleep."

"Pitney, are you coming?" The officer on the deck sounded impatient.

"On my way, sir." Jefferson Pitney gave Becky a smile and a little salute before returning up the ladder to the main deck, and she turned red once more.

"He's a know-it-all," remarked Patrick after the older boy had left. Becky only frowned at her brother.

"Why do you say that? I like him." Michael had the bear cub on a leash. "Let's go up on the deck and watch Dublin disappear."

Several hours later the spires and smoke of Dublin had faded behind them in a fresh, following breeze. Only a blue smudge on the horizon still reminded Patrick that his home was somewhere in the distance. His mother sniffed at the wind and smiled down at him with tears in her eyes.

"I can still see Bray Head." She pointed to a distant rise in the land, a city crowned with hills that he had never seen from this direction. "And there's Big and Little Sugarloaf . . . and War Hill . . . and Sally Gap. . . . See?"

Patrick nodded, staying safely away from the ship's railing, as far away from the foamy green fingers of the Irish Sea as he could manage. It was cold out there, and he couldn't seem to get the knot out of his throat.

"I'm going to miss—" he began, but his voice caught in his throat.

"Me too, Patrick." His mother put her arm around his shoulder. "But if this means we'll be closer to your father, it will be home for me."

Above Patrick's head he could hear a faint humming of the wind through the rigging and the occasional shouts of a sailor as another row of sails was unfurled. A seagull had followed them out of the harbor, but it finally tired and turned back. Below Patrick's feet the deck dipped and swayed in time to the waves.

Do we really know what we're doing? he worried.

CHAPTER 9

THE SOUTHERN CROSS

Patrick knew he would never forget their first month at sea. With no way to escape the ship's endless rocking, the waves at first made him dizzy, then worse. At least below decks he could hide from the winds that sliced the foaming tops off the waves and buffed his skin until his hands and cheeks were raw and bleeding. But he could never escape his first thought every morning as he huddled in his damp canvas bunk.

Am I still alive?

Of course he was, day after day and week after week. February finally arrived. To help pass the time, he tried to read a couple of dog-eared books from the captain's collection, stories like *Oliver Twist* by Charles Dickens (with only a couple of pages missing) or a biography of the American frontiersman, Davy Crockett (which he enjoyed). Mostly, though, he found himself sitting at the dining-room table inside the ship's salon, staring out a porthole and watching the endless parade of long, rolling waves.

There's never any land, he thought as the stars were coming out one night. *Just waves and more waves.*

"Patrick?" Becky interrupted his thoughts when she poked her head down from the deck. "Are you still here? Ma was wondering about you."

"Nothing to wonder." He leaned back on the wooden bench next to the table and rested his head against the shelf behind him. "I've just been reading."

"So why don't you come up on deck? You've been moping for days. You'll feel better."

Patrick turned over a page, sighed, and slammed his book shut.

"Come on," she urged him again. "The wind has calmed down."

Patrick nodded weakly and climbed up the stair ladder to the deck.

"It's getting too dark to read anyway," he admitted.

"See?" Becky asked him. "Isn't it beautiful?"

When he looked around, Patrick had to admit the evening was like nothing he had ever seen. The air was soft and almost alive with the deep, dark red-orange of a fading sunset, and the wind had settled down to a friendly, constant murmur from behind. Above them the sails filled out like fluffy pillows. Their mother and Michael were standing at the railing and had their heads back to watch the stars pop out in the inky sky.

Becky looked up, too. "Jefferson said that since we're close to the equator, we'll start seeing different stars than we're used to. Just like the seasons will change. On the other side of the equator, winter is summer, and summer is winter."

Patrick frowned in the shadows when he heard Jefferson Pitney's name, but the early evening was too beautiful to worry about the know-it-all cabin boy. He put his hands up to his eyes like blinders to see better.

"Come over here, Patrick," his mother called to him. "I want to show you something."

Patrick looked down for a moment and stepped carefully over to join them.

"Look up that way in the sky. What do you see?"

He followed the direction his mother pointed to study a faint, glimmering cluster of stars. The McWaids stood staring for a while, letting the warm breeze wash over them.

"The Southern Cross," his mother finally explained. "If you drew a line between them, those four bright stars would look just like—"

"A cross!" Michael interrupted. "Now I see it, Ma."

Patrick did, too, and his mother continued.

"And I understand from the captain that if you follow a line down from the top star to the bottom one, the line will lead you almost straight south."

"That's where we're going to find Pa." Michael sounded as if he had everything figured out. "We just keep going straight south."

"I wish it were that simple," Patrick whispered. The Southern Cross went blurry as he stared up at the sky through his tears. He quickly wiped his eyes with the sleeve of his sweater and turned away so no one would see.

"What happens if . . ." he began, and then he couldn't stop the words from tumbling out. "How do we—what are we going to do when we get there without . . ."

They stood there together quietly, just the four of them, Patrick with his unfinished question. Except for knowing his mother and brother and sister were right next to him, he had never felt more alone in his life. Patrick was sure they all knew what he had meant to—but couldn't—say.

"What are we going to do without your pa?" Their mother's voice was quiet, but she held on to them even more tightly.

"I think about it all the time, Patrick," she went on. Her voice sounded gentle. "And I'm scared, too, going to a strange land, where we don't know a soul. All I know is that God is making a way for us, and we just have to get as close to your pa as we can."

She took a deep breath. "And you know what? Your brother was right."

"I was?" Michael seemed surprised.

"Yes, you were," she told him. "Because all we can do is just keep going . . . and follow that cross."

Follow that cross. It sounded like something his pastor would have said during a sermon back home in their church in Dublin. Patrick wasn't sure how his mother had meant it, but when he looked up at the gathering stars, "following that cross" seemed to make all the sense in the world.

At least it gave them a nightly event for the next few weeks as

March approached. Something to look forward to in the warm evenings as the sun set, when the sky was clear. Patrick and his brother would even have contests to see who could find the cross first. Michael usually won. Once in a while even Jefferson Pitney would play along if he wasn't busy climbing the mast or mending sails. But when he did, Patrick usually found something else to do.

"The star's real name is *crux*," explained the older boy in a tone of voice that reminded Patrick of a professor making a long-winded speech. "That's Latin for . . ."

Patrick groaned and went below, leaving Michael and Becky to the Latin lecture. *Only twenty more days with Jefferson Pitney*, he told himself. *If I can last that long*.

CHAPTER 10

THE RED COAST

"Are we almost there, Patrick?" asked Michael. After a plain breakfast of lukewarm porridge, the brothers and Becky were taking the captain's bear for a morning walk around the deck. "We *have* to be there by now. We've been on this ship all my life."

"Seems like it, doesn't it?" Patrick slowed down so he wouldn't trip over the bear. "But you can count as well as anyone else, Michael. It's April, and we've been at sea eighty-three days. It's supposed to take eighty-five days to reach Australia, if you can believe Jefferson. That leaves us—"

Michael made a show of counting on his fingers as Jefferson walked their direction. The cabin boy was carrying a leaky wooden bucket and a well-worn scrub brush.

"Only one more day till we see Pa!" exclaimed Michael.

"No kidding?" The cabin boy put down his bucket to scratch Ebony. "Say, I've been meaning to ask you. Y'all have talked about your pa this whole trip, but why haven't you ever told me what he's doing in Australia?"

Patrick shrugged and tried to move on, but the bear wouldn't budge. "You never asked."

"So does he work for the government or something like that?"

"Sort of."

71

Patrick would have left it at that, but Becky came up behind him.

"Patrick, you can't say that. We can't keep it a secret."

"Why not?" He didn't turn around.

"Because . . . well, we just can't, that's all. Jefferson was only asking."

Patrick crossed his arms and frowned, not saying anything else. Off to the side, the early morning sun slowly lit up the eastern sky.

"You should know, Jeff." Becky stepped around her brother. "Our pa's a prisoner."

"But he didn't do anything wrong," Michael added quickly.

As if he couldn't believe it, Jefferson shook his head while Becky and Michael told him their story. Patrick added a little about the trial, but they didn't mention Conrad Burke by name. Not even Becky wanted to talk about *him*.

"And all this time you kept it a secret."

Becky looked down. "I'm sorry. We didn't know what to say. Now we're just hoping we'll get to see him, or visit him, soon."

"I think you will."

"You do?" Becky sounded hopeful.

"Sure. It's not like they keep prisoners in cells all the time. In fact . . ."

Patrick's mind started to wander as Jefferson Pitney launched into another of his stories. The waves caught his attention as the morning sky turned the water from inky purple to yellow and everything in between. This morning, something seemed different.

"Are those clouds out there?" Patrick interrupted, and Jefferson looked annoyed.

"I don't think so." Becky glanced for a moment into the distance and wrinkled her nose. A huge gray-and-white seagull cried overhead, as if scolding them for trespassing on his patch of ocean.

Michael noticed the bird and jumped to his feet. "We haven't seen a bird like that since we left South Africa." Then he cupped his hands and shouted into the wind. "Hello, bird! Come down here!"

That's when it dawned on Patrick. He held his hands up like a telescope and looked more carefully at the clouds in the distance.

"Those aren't just clouds," he told them, his voice raising several notches. "That's Australia!"

Shouts from men in the rigging overhead told Patrick that he was right.

"Ma!" Becky scurried below to tell their mother while Michael and Patrick jumped up and down.

"See?" Michael hung on to his older brother's shoulders as he jumped. "All we had to do was follow the Southern Cross. I told you!"

Patrick let himself smile for the first time in days. It felt good.

Jefferson was quickly called to his station in the forward part of the ship as the rest of the sailors hurried to their jobs.

"Step lively, boys," yelled one of the officers. "We'll be in Fremantle before you know."

Even though the wind grew stronger all the time, the next hours seemed to drag more slowly than ever as they surfed closer to the barren red coast. Patrick and Becky took turns eagerly scanning the distance with the captain's telescope, looking for buildings, trees, people—anything that would tell them this was really Australia.

"I still don't see anything," reported Michael, shading his eyes against the water's glare. "Only beaches and rocks."

Jefferson laughed as he hurried back to where they were standing. "We'll be lucky if we don't fetch up on those beaches and rocks," answered Jefferson. He held out his hand for the telescope. "Here, the captain will need this if we're going to make it into Fremantle. The passage is a bit tricky."

Patrick kept his eye on the land as they turned, his mother standing next to him, crossing and uncrossing her arms. They held on for balance as the ship scooted closer toward the sunburned land.

"He's there," said Becky. "I know he's there."

"Sure he's there," answered Patrick, "but I still don't know how our plan is going to work. Do we go live in the prison with him?"

"You're worrying again, Patrick." Becky kept her eyes on the coast. "Jefferson says most of the prisoners are sent out to work. Sometimes a prisoner will even get to live and work at a ranch."

"Jefferson says." Patrick wrinkled his nose.

"Does that mean we could live at the same place where Pa has to work?" Michael looked hopeful, and his mother put her hand on his shoulder.

"I don't know, dear. We just need to find out where he is and what he's doing. Then wait and see."

"This is where we're going to live?" Patrick looked around as the ship slowly made its way into the harbor a day after they had first sighted land. "There's nothing here but a couple of old ships and that . . ." He wasn't sure what to call the long, low white building overlooking the sea.

"This is Fremantle," answered one of the sailors. "And those are the convict barracks. They call it The Establishment. You don't want to go there."

Oh yes, I do, Patrick thought to himself as Jefferson rowed out with one of the ship's anchors. When the small boat was far enough ahead, Jeff dropped the anchor straight down into the waters of the harbor, and sailors on the forward deck cranked in the chain by winding it around a large spool. They repeated the process several times before getting close enough to the pier to tie up.

"See the name on that ship?" asked Becky, jumping up and down. She gave her brother a smug grin. "I knew he would be here. Remember how much we've prayed?"

"H-o-u . . ." began Michael.

"Hougoumont." Jefferson finished the word for him, then looked at Becky. "Good luck finding him."

"I'm going straight to the barracks," declared Patrick.

Michael jumped up and down. "Pa's going to be surprised."

"Don't you boys go running away," warned their mother. "We've come halfway around the world. We're going to stay together."

Even in the dry heat, the men worked quickly to secure their ship at the primitive dock. Patrick strained to catch a glimpse of any life, especially near the prison buildings or on the *Hougoumont*.

"Looks as if it's a ghost town." Becky straightened her hair, which had grown longer and lighter during their weeks at sea.

Forgetting what his mother had told him, Patrick didn't listen for more. *Almost here, Pa.* When the ship was only a few feet from the pier, he slipped to the rear deck and leaped. Rotting timbers gave way as he landed, and a moment later he found himself dangling over the water by his elbows.

"Ow!" He felt splinters in his legs, but no one on the ship noticed except a sailor pulling thick rope through an opening in the waist-high railing. Somehow it didn't matter.

"Hey, now, we'll be there soon enough," said the sailor, but Patrick had already pulled himself up.

"Patrick!" he heard Becky call, and he motioned for her to follow.

"Come on!" he called back as he sprinted past a long-bearded man pulling a cart.

"Watch yourself!" the man cried out, nearly steering his cart into the bay.

"Excuse me," Patrick called back. He could hear another pair of footsteps on the pier behind him.

"Which way, do you think?" he asked over his shoulder.

"I don't know, Patrick," replied his sister. "Ask that fellow over there."

Becky pointed to a man in a faded red jacket sitting at a table outside the open front door of the prison barracks. He looked bored, but at least he sat in the shade of an old canvas sail someone had put up as an awning over his outdoor office.

"Where do you think you're going?" he asked as they ran across a lane and up to the table. The man spoke with an unusual accent, not English, not American like Jefferson, but with a definite twang that had to be Australian.

For a moment Patrick couldn't answer. After living on the ship for almost three months, his legs seemed like wet noodles, and his lungs burned as he sucked in the hot, dry, dust-filled air. And even though they were finally on dry land, everything seemed to rock below him more than ever.

"We're here to see John McWaid, please," said Patrick's mother, hurrying up behind them with Michael in tow. She must have run almost as fast as Becky and Patrick after the gangplank had come down. "We've come all the way from—"

"From Ireland," interrupted the man, waving away a small swarm of flies from his face. "I can hear that. Wait a minute."

The soldier leafed casually through his ledger book, the kind accountants used to write long columns of numbers.

"McWaid," repeated Becky eagerly. "Is he in this building?"

The man didn't answer, only licked his finger and leafed through another section of his book.

"Jenkins!" he called over his shoulder. When a younger soldier arrived, the man with the book whispered something in his ear and pointed to an entry on a fly-specked page. Patrick tried to read upside down but could see nothing more than a scribbled note next to a name that had been crossed out. Finally the clerk looked up.

"He's not here. You'll need to inquire with the on-duty officer of the *Hougoumont*. Some of the officers are still aboard, waiting for the next assignment."

"Not here?" stuttered Mrs. McWaid. "But that can't be."

"That's all I can tell you," insisted the man, slamming his book shut with a flourish and a little cloud of dust. "If he's not in this book, he's not here." He went back to adding a long row of figures.

Patrick's mother stood, her face looking confused, her arms around Michael and Becky.

"Are you saying he was never here, or that he was here and already left?" Patrick remembered what the guards had been like back in Ireland, and he wasn't giving up so easily. The clerk looked to the uniformed guard who stood stiffly behind him.

"Corporal, would you show these people back to wherever they came from?" he barked.

Before the soldier could move, Patrick's mother turned and guided her children away from the table. Patrick had the feeling they had been through this before, back at the Kilmainham Jail in Dublin. Only now, where was their father?

"Come on, children," she told them gently. "Perhaps your father is still down on that ship."

"Ship's being readied to sail, ma'am," said the young guard, who had come from behind the table. He walked them back out to the dusty street, away from the building, and lowered his voice. "I'm not sure why Sergeant Wilkinson told you to go back there."

"You mean it's empty?" Patrick couldn't believe it.

The guard shrugged and looked back at the barracks. "They don't tell me anything. But I saw the last of the prisoners taken out of that ship weeks ago."

"All of them?" asked Becky.

The soldier swallowed hard and stopped in his tracks. "I have to get back to my post. Good day to you."

The foursome marched back the way they had come, this time heading directly to the ragged-looking ship called the *Hougoumont*. Patrick stopped for a second before climbing aboard. Was his father in chains?

Only a few sailors lazed around the deck, but Mrs. McWaid marched up to the nearest one.

"Can you tell us where to find your officers?" she inquired.

The sailor didn't get to his feet, only nodded his head toward the main cabin. "First mate's in there, but he's been . . ." A slow grin crept across the young man's face, and he didn't finish his sentence. "Aw, go ahead, ma'am. In there."

"In there" was the dark, rank inside of a main cabin that smelled as if something dead had been left to rot. It took a moment for Patrick's eyes to adjust to the darkness.

"Hello?" called Becky. Her mother eased past her to stand in the doorway. They heard a grunt and a chair scraping. "Is anyone here?"

A middle-aged man in a wrinkled blue uniform stood unsteadily before them, bowing slightly before nearly tumbling on his head. He pulled himself back up with his right hand.

"First Officer Simmons, here. To whom do I owe the honor?"

he began, his breath hitting them like the foul air of a pub. Patrick flinched; he had smelled it too many times before, back in the streets of Dublin.

"I'm Sarah McWaid," began Patrick's mother, taking a step back. Becky gripped her mother's arm for safety, and Michael hid behind her skirt for protection. Patrick stood ready to either run or protect the others, he wasn't sure which.

"We are looking for my husband," continued his mother. "He was brought here to Australia on this ship. But the officer at the barracks said he wasn't there, and that we should inquire with you."

"Oh, he did, did he?" drawled the officer. "So you're here with that Irish newspaper fellow—what was his name . . . Burke?" He wheeled around and motioned to a bench next to the dining table.

"Conrad Burke?" asked Patrick, his mind stunned at the mention of the name. *There has to be some mistake!*

The man stopped, as if remembering something.

"Do you know Conrad Burke?" Becky pressed him.

He can't be here, Patrick fumed. *Isn't it good enough for him that Pa's a prisoner? Why would he come here?*

"No . . . eh, he's not here anymore." The man waved off the question. "And it's no concern of yours. Have a seat, won't you?"

Mrs. McWaid didn't move. "Thank you very much, but I'll stand."

"Wait a minute," insisted Patrick. He felt the hairs on the back of his neck stand on end. "You mentioned Burke. Why won't you tell us—"

"Patrick!" His mother cut him off. "Don't talk to the man that way."

The man gazed back at her with a bland smile, then sat down with a sigh. "Quite all right. So tell me which poor wretch you might be looking for, or rather why you bother. You didn't come all the way from Ireland just to follow a prisoner, did you?"

"John McWaid," she blurted out. "We're looking for John McWaid. Do you know him?"

For a moment the man stiffened, just as the officer at the barracks had done, but then he relaxd again and put on a gravely serious look. "McWaid, you say?"

The first mate shouted for another sailor and whispered something in his ear. *What are they all whispering about?* wondered Patrick. The sailor nodded and slipped away again into the shadows of the dark room.

"Mrs. McWaid, you're going to want to sit down," the officer advised her. He tried to straighten his shirt.

"Why won't someone tell me what's happened to my husband?" Their mother was growing upset, but she held her ground by the door.

"Mrs. McWaid, I'm afraid your husband . . . ah . . . died on the voyage here to Australia."

Their mother gasped, and Patrick couldn't believe what his ears told him. *Not after all this! Not after all our praying!*

"The ship's surgeon tells me it was due to consumption," continued the man. "Perfectly dreadful in the tropics. I was personally in charge of the burial. We were in the middle of the Indian Ocean at the time, several weeks back."

Patrick's mother buried her face in her hands and fell to her knees. Becky hugged her, and Michael looked at Patrick with tears in his eyes. Patrick still didn't believe the officer.

A nightmare, he thought. *I'm going to wake up, and it will all be over.*

"Are you sure it was my father?" Patrick heard himself say. "What did he look like?"

The officer's voice was now quiet and low, as if he were trying to comfort them. "Powerful build, curly red hair. . . . He was one of four prisoners who passed away. I'm sorry to be the one to tell you."

Still Patrick would not believe it, and the only thing he could think of was getting away from the horrible prison ship. With his mind in a confused fog, he pushed past Michael, ran out on deck, and vaulted back to the old pier.

"Patrick!" his sister called after him, but this time he wouldn't, couldn't, stop. He ran from the pier, through the streets of sleeping dogs, past the prison barracks. He ran as fast as his aching legs would carry him, and when his legs gave out, he tumbled into a dusty side street. A pack of three or four hungry-looking dogs followed, sniffing curiously. By that time his eyes would not hold back the tears any longer.

Patrick wasn't sure how long he sat in the dusty alley crying. At last Becky found him.

"There you are," she said gently. Patrick couldn't see her through his tears, but the voice he recognized. He felt like a little boy, but he couldn't stop crying. Becky kneeled in the dust with him, her arm around his shoulder.

"We have to go back and see Ma," she told him after a minute. Her eyes were red, too.

"Let me just—" he gasped. "Let me just catch my b-b-breath."

Becky nodded and Patrick tried to stand again. When he turned around, though, their way was blocked by a young sailor. The same sailor who had been called into the first mate's room on the prison ship!

"Listen," he croaked, looking nervously over his shoulder before slipping up next to them. One of the dogs crept closer and sniffed Patrick curiously.

"Your father's not dead," whispered the sailor before Patrick and Becky could say anything. He bit his lip. "At least not yet."

"What do you mean?" gasped Becky, scrambling to her feet. The sailor looked around once more, as if the dogs were spies.

"Just what I said. We buried four men at sea, but none of them had curly red hair."

"Are you sure?" asked Patrick.

The sailor spat in disgust. "This trip I had the job of burying four people at sea. None of them was named John McWaid. Understand what I'm saying?"

Patrick looked at his sister in confusion. "Why would the officer tell us that Pa was dead if he wasn't?"

"I don't know what First Officer Simmons told you. All I'm saying is that we didn't bury your pa at sea."

The way he spit out the officer's name told Patrick that the two were not the best of friends.

"What are you saying?" asked Patrick.

The sailor shrugged. "Just this: Your father's not in the prison barracks here, and he's not on the ship."

"You mean he's escaped?" whispered Becky.

"I didn't tell you that." But it was obvious that was exactly what the young sailor was trying to tell them. "Nobody else will, either, if he wants to keep his job. A prisoner escapes, and you say something else happened. 'He died,' you might say. It looks better that way. Understand?"

"Why would he escape, though?" wondered Patrick. "Isn't that dangerous?"

The sailor shrugged. "No more dangerous than staying where they don't want you alive, if you know what I mean."

Patrick was getting used to the roundabout way this nervous man was telling them the story.

"But who?" he asked. "Who wanted to hurt Pa?"

The sailor shook his head furiously. "I've already told you more than I should. All I can say is that he disappeared somehow when we were unloading the ship. They searched for days, but even the dogs found nothing."

"So what does that mean?" asked Becky. "You must tell us."

The sailor pointed past a building to the scrubby underbrush and the low, parched hills that surrounded the town. "Nobody survives out there in the outback except the natives," he continued. Patrick guessed the man meant the aborigines, the black natives of this land that some of the sailors on the ship had told them about. "Can't live for long on snakes and bugs."

Patrick nodded seriously.

"My opinion is that your father either died out there in the bush, or else somebody helped him slip out on the *Great Victoria*."

"A ship?" asked Patrick.

The sailor nodded. "Passed through here just before anyone

discovered your father was gone. Headed east, Adelaide way—maybe Sydney."

"Have you ever heard of Conrad Burke?" Becky tried one more question.

The sailor paused for a moment, and his eyes narrowed. "If you mean that crazy newspaper fella, he's still out there, looking for the prisoner. But he's wasting his time. And now I've told you too much."

"But—" began Patrick, but the sailor grabbed him by the collar.

"That's all I'm saying, and you don't breathe a word of any of it, understand? You just get back on your ship and leave this place straightaway. Forget you ever came here."

Patrick and his sister both nodded. The young man, apparently satisfied, spun on his heel and slipped away without another word. When he reached the street, he checked it carefully, then crossed his arms and sauntered casually out into the full midday sun. A final warning look over his shoulder was enough to convince them.

"Think he's telling the truth?" Patrick asked his sister.

"I do. And I have a feeling we don't want to be here in Fremantle when Burke comes back."

CHAPTER 11

THE TEST

"Come on, Patrick, Pa's not back there. Remember?" Becky tried to cheer up her brother again as he stared at the waves behind them. It had taken the men on the *Star of Africa* only a day and a half to load fresh water and provisions aboard before they had been sent on their way once again. Now more than a week later, they had scooted around the southern coast of the island continent of Australia on their way to the next port, Adelaide.

Patrick nodded. "I hope you're right. I just wish Pa knew we're trying to find him."

"Me too." Becky shuddered as they stood on deck. "But at least we didn't run into . . ."

Her voice trailed off, and Patrick was glad she didn't mention Conrad Burke. He didn't want to think about what might have happened if the man had returned while they were still in Fremantle. And he still didn't feel up to explaining it all to Jefferson.

The cabin boy coiled a rope in his hands and steadied himself against the pitching deck. "I say it was decent of the navy fellows back in Fremantle to pay your way to Adelaide."

"Decent?" Patrick frowned. "I don't think Ma had a choice. Simmons ordered us out of there."

He grabbed for a handhold as their ship pitched through another wave. Back out at sea it was rougher than ever, and Patrick's stomach wasn't letting him forget it. But his only other choice was to stay down below, where everyone else was sick, too.

"The only thing to do now is catch up with the *Great Victoria* or find our grandfather and get him to help us," explained Becky.

"This is the grandfather you've never met, right?"

Becky nodded. Patrick still didn't like the way Jefferson was talking to his sister, close and with a smile, so he slipped in between the two.

"Ma thinks Pa would try to find Grandpa, too," put in Michael, who was watching the seabirds that were following them. "All we have to do is find that town with the funny name and ask around, see if he still lives there."

"If he ever did," Patrick reminded him.

Jefferson backed away. "Echuca, you mean. Lots of towns have odd names in Australia. There's Wollongong and Toowoomba, BurraBurra. . . ."

Patrick almost laughed, then painted a frown back on his face. He was supposed to be protecting his sister from this sailor, not laughing at his jokes.

"How do you know all that?" asked Michael.

The older boy smiled knowingly and tapped his head. "I remember maps. All I have to do is look at them once and—"

"Pitney, get up here!" yelled a sailor from the rigging above. The ship pitched headfirst into a deep trough between two waves, throwing Patrick to his knees on the deck. Jefferson was ready, though; with one hand on the rigging, he grabbed Becky around the shoulders to keep her from tumbling, too.

"Thank you." She smiled at the older boy, and he didn't let her go right away. Patrick scrambled to his feet and grabbed his sister's hand.

"Come on, Becky." Another wave sent a shower of spray over the deck, soaking Michael first. "It's getting too rough up here. We have to go downstairs."

"Your brother's right," agreed Jefferson, waving up at the sailor who had called to him from the rigging. "I have to go up and help take down a sail. You'll be safer below."

When they had made it to the bottom of the stairway of the main cabin, Michael gripped his chest and fluttered his eyebrows at his older sister. "You'll be safer below, sweetheart," he chirped. "Save yourself, my love."

Becky only batted away his teasing with a swat to his ear, but he ducked before she could catch him. Another wave sent a shudder down the ship's spine, and they all had to hold on to keep their balance.

"I'm glad you children came below when you did," their mother shouted over the howling of the wind. She gestured for them to sit with her at the main dining table. "Otherwise I was coming up for you."

Patrick struggled to close the double doors behind him, and with his sister's help they got them secured. No one could eat in the rough waters, so they gripped the table and tried to sing hymns as the afternoon wore on. They sang as many verses as they could remember of "Oh, for a Thousand Tongues," then the chorus of "On Christ the Solid Rock I Stand," which everyone seemed to remember better, and "Stand Up, Stand Up for Jesus."

"Speaking of standing up," their mother finally said, struggling to rise. "I'm sorry, children, I . . ." Her face had turned pale, and she excused herself. The pitching and rocking was becoming worse.

"I'm not feeling too well, either," admitted Becky, following her mother forward. Patrick and Michael were the only ones left in the main salon.

"I'm not sure what's worse," Patrick told his brother after a while. "Sitting down here getting sick, or standing up on deck getting sick."

Michael squeezed his lips tightly together and hugged his arms to his stomach. "I think I'll go check on Ebony. He's probably scared."

Patrick sat alone at the dining-room table for a few minutes, trying to hum a few choruses. Things in the cabin rolled around.

This is the roughest it's ever been, he told himself. *And we're close to shore*. Once in a while he heard shouts from sailors out on deck, but only as the wind seemed to hurl the words through the air his way. Every so often he could feel the ship rear back to climb a wave, and everything in the main salon would clatter to one side. Up, up, up they would climb, the wind shrieking in the rigging above like some kind of wild, out-of-tune violin. Finally they would pause, shudder, and race back down the far side of the wave, and everything would crash back to the other side of the shelves. Several dishes smashed to pieces on the wood floor at the other end of the salon. Patrick caught a book as it scooted past him on the floor.

Still the crew battled the waves outside. Patrick felt as if he were riding a giant rocking horse, until a stray wave caught the ship from the side and shook him silly. His stomach started to protest. Patrick glanced quickly around, but the only thing he could think of was to crawl out on deck before he got sick.

Just for a minute, he told himself. *Maybe the fresh air will help*.

As soon as he undid the latch, though, a fierce wind caught the main doors and slammed them open. Patrick was nearly sucked up the short stairway and out on the heaving deck. He dug his fingernails into a wooden railing and looked down as his feet were buried ankle-deep in boiling foam.

Slowly he fought his way to the edge of the railing, his fears temporarily overruled by the horrible feeling in his stomach. Only suddenly the ocean wasn't content to stay in its place—it was all over the ship, washing down the decks and filling the air with stinging sheets of spray. Moving walls of green water tried to knock him to his knees.

"Hold—" someone yelled from above, but the rest of what the sailor shouted was torn from his mouth by the howling wind.

Patrick looked up for a moment at the struggling figures in oilskins, wrestling with a ripped, flapping sail. One of them looked familiar, and he recognized Jefferson, whose hood had blown back away from his face. When the older boy saw Patrick on deck, his expression turned even darker than the clouds overhead.

"What?" Patrick yelled back. He could see Jefferson's mouth moving but could catch only a few of the words.

"You . . . back . . . below. Now!" hollered Jefferson, pointing at the door to the main cabin. He started climbing back down the rope ladder on the side of the main mast when a particularly vicious wave grabbed the ship and knocked it on its ear.

The wave must have caught Jefferson off guard because the next thing Patrick knew, he saw the older boy hanging from his feet in the rigging, waving like a piece of ripped sailcloth.

"Jefferson!" screamed Patrick, but no one else saw or heard.

A moment later the older boy's ankle slipped out of the rope ladder. He bumped past the ship's railing, crumpled into a ball, and dropped headfirst into the waves.

CHAPTER 12

A WATERY ENEMY

"No!" Patrick forgot about his seasickness as he watched Jefferson's body wash away behind them. He looked around in panic to see who would help. A couple of men were up forward, but their backs were turned. Not even the man who was struggling with the ship's giant steering wheel had seen the accident.

By the time they got the ship turned around—*if* they could get it turned around—Jefferson would be gone. *What if he was knocked out by the fall?*

There was only one thing to do, Patrick thought as he ripped a life ring off the railing.

"Hey, Helmsman!" he screamed at the top of his lungs. "Man overboard!"

The man at the wheel never looked back, but Patrick launched out over the railing with the life ring clutched tightly in his hands. There wasn't time for anything else.

Here I go, Lord, Patrick prayed as he pedaled his legs in the air on the way down to the water. *I can't let him drown, too. Not like Sean. Please, I just can't—*

Patrick's prayer was cut short by the crush of salt water slapping him in the face. For a moment he thought he would lose the life ring, but he refused to let go and started kicking. At least the water wasn't cold, especially when he was out of the wind.

"Jefferson!" he hollered, pushing the large cork ring in front of him as he would a raft. The *Star of Africa* would turn around. It had to. But first he would have to reach Jefferson before he drowned. Was that his head bobbing up ahead in the gray late-afternoon light?

"Where are you?" Patrick shouted into the face of the wind. He sputtered as spray from the top of a wave hit him full in the face. Something in the distance had looked like a waving hand, then disappeared. Suddenly he knew how terribly tiny and helpless he was.

What have I done? he asked himself. The face of his youngest brother, Sean, floated before him. Instead of the Indian Ocean, he felt as if he were back home, standing helplessly on that bridge over the River Liffey.

"Sean!" he called before a mouthful of seawater snapped him back to reality. "I mean, Jefferson!"

Calling Jefferson's name over and over, Patrick surfed down one wave and climbed up the next. He knew he couldn't swim against the waves, but if they carried him, maybe he had a chance. All he could do was pray that he was drifting in the right direction.

"Over here!" came a weak voice. For an instant Patrick caught sight of Jefferson's white face, only two waves away.

"Hold on," Patrick pleaded, but the wind seemed to snatch the words from his mouth. "Just hold on. Please . . ."

He saw Jefferson's frightened face again. They were doing a horrible up-and-down dance, each caught on twin wave tops. Patrick put his face down and kicked hard.

"I'm not going to let you win again," he threatened the sea, but the water only made him choke. He gasped for air and looked up to see a wild-eyed Jefferson Pitney grabbing desperately at the big life ring.

"Where did you come from?" sputtered the cabin boy.

Patrick looked back toward the ship as they bobbed from wave to wave.

"Didn't anyone . . . see me fall?" Jefferson wiped the hair away from his dark eyes and held on to the back of his head. His hand came away red.

"I don't know. But you sure banged your head on the way down."

Jefferson took note of the blood and winced in pain. "Didn't notice it until just now."

"Shouldn't they be turning around?" Patrick squinted back at the ship.

"They'll have a hard time turning back into the wind. But you shouldn't have jumped after me. That was a stupid thing to do."

"I had to." Patrick was sure of that. Even if no one would ever understand why, he knew it was the only thing he could have done.

Jefferson felt at the gash in the back of his head once more. Still bleeding. "There's no use in both of us . . ."

He didn't need to finish his sentence. As they bobbed crazily in the powerful waves, the *Star of Africa* grew smaller and smaller until it finally disappeared behind the waves.

"I should have made sure they saw me jump," whispered Patrick, the emotion drained from his voice.

For the next few hours they hung on in silence. There was not much use trying to talk above the crash of the waves. And there was no sunset, only a darker and darker gray.

"Still there?" Patrick cleared his throat when it was completely dark. At least his stomach wasn't sick, as it had been on the ship.

Jefferson didn't answer.

"Jefferson? Come on, answer me!"

"Here," the older boy replied in a glum voice.

"How long can you hang on?"

"Long as I have to," Jefferson paused. "But listen, I still have my knife. I'll cut off the line from around this ring. Tie one end around your wrist and the other to the ring."

Patrick obeyed, making sure not to tie the rope too tightly. His hands were starting to feel raw from trying to hold on to the canvas and cork.

"You think there are any sharks out here?" Patrick wondered aloud.

"Plenty. But I'm not too worried about them."

"Why not?"

"The waves. The sharks will keep away—at least until it's calm."

"What then?"

"Then they'll follow my blood."

There was a ripping sound from Jefferson's direction. Patrick guessed it had to be a piece of clothing.

"What are you doing now?"

Jefferson didn't answer.

"Jefferson?"

"I'm trying to stop the bleeding, of course. Somebody didn't tell them about the waves."

"What do you mean, *them*?" Patrick caught his breath.

"Sharks. I just felt a shark brush by."

Patrick struggled to hug his knees to his chest.

"Are you sure?" He could hardly hear his own whisper. "I thought you said—"

"Would you quit asking so many questions? It's still too dark to tell. Just don't move."

Patrick wanted to do what Jefferson told him, but the more he tried to stay still, the more he shivered.

"You can pray, too," commanded Jefferson. "Not that I think it's going to do us any good, but go ahead."

Patrick didn't have a chance to answer before something brushed against his leg. Something big and rough.

"Oh!" Patrick couldn't keep from calling out in the darkness. He grabbed the life ring even more tightly. If he could have, he would have shot straight out of the water.

"I said hold still!" Jefferson barked.

"I . . . I c-can't!" Patrick managed through chattering teeth. Something splashed behind him, then something strong and hard bumped him on the ankle.

"Another one!" Jefferson yelled, slapping at the water with a piece of rope before the sea turned to foam between them. Patrick screamed in fright as a set of gleaming white teeth took hold of their life ring. It jerked out of his grip.

"Hey!" Tied by his wrist to the life ring, Patrick could do nothing but grab for it.

"No!" Jefferson gasped as they thrashed in the water.

Patrick closed his eyes and kicked as hard as he could, his toe meeting what he guessed was the shark's belly.

This is it, God, he prayed, kicking again with all his might. *The next thing I'll feel is—*

The shark gave their ring another jerk, then everything was still.

"Jefferson?" Patrick was afraid to touch the life ring, afraid to open his eyes, afraid to breathe. He wasn't completely sure he was still alive. But he gasped for air anyway, almost not expecting the other boy to answer.

"I'm still here. It's gone—for now."

Patrick sighed with relief and tried to keep from crying. He felt along the life ring. Despite a few jagged tooth marks, it was still floating.

"Looks as if the shark didn't like the taste of our life ring," reported Jefferson. "He could have bitten it in two if he'd a mind to."

"I s-suppose."

"If he comes back, though, he won't spit *us* out the way he did the cork."

Patrick didn't answer. He just held on as the hours passed, thinking about what it would be like to find Pa and to be together with Becky and Michael and Ma again. He felt through his shirt for his grandmother's ring, still hanging around his neck. He wanted to cry, but instead he prayed, not caring if Jefferson heard him or not.

"Little late for that," drawled Jefferson. "I haven't heard so much prayin' since I was back home in Arkansas."

"I thought you wanted me to pray." Patrick kept his feet up in case the sharks returned. "Don't you believe in prayer?"

"Never have before. Never had a reason to."

"Really?" Patrick took a breath, irritated for a moment that Jefferson would talk that way after everything they had just been through. "Well, now you *do* have a reason to pray. You're alive."

Patrick wasn't used to talking about prayer to anyone. Sure, his family had prayed a lot, especially after Pa had been imprisoned.

With Ma and Pa, though, it had been different and safe. Now he was on his own.

"Hmmph," Jefferson answered. "I still think it was a fool thing for you to come after me. But I owe you if we make it to land."

"You don't owe *me*." Patrick was suddenly sure of himself as he looked toward the sky. Even though he couldn't see the bright Southern Cross through the clouds, he knew it was there. "And we *will* make it."

"Hey, kid! Can't be snoozing."

Patrick woke to a splash of salt water in the face. His armpits were chapped from hanging on and rubbing against the life ring, his lips felt bloated, and his throat was almost swollen shut. But when he opened his eyes, Jefferson Pitney was grinning at him.

"Oh, it's you." Each word stung as it came out. "Don't call me kid."

"Sure, kid." Jefferson motioned with his head. "But look out that way. Maybe there's something to that prayin' of yours after all."

Patrick followed the older boy's gaze. The wind was still blowing, but the monstrous waves from the night before had settled down into long, powerful rollers that propelled them toward a hazy blue shore. He blinked his stinging eyes. He could barely make out a row of tall, jagged cliffs, crowned by an untidy growth of scrub.

"What place is that?" he croaked as the sun peeked over the land's crown.

Jefferson shook his head. "Won't matter at all to me as long as it doesn't rock and sway. If we both paddle, we'll be there in no time."

Three hours later Patrick gave up trying to shade his sunburned forehead. He studied the land and noticed something far down the coastline, to their left.

"Is that a lighthouse up on the cliff?" he asked. It still hurt to talk.

"I noticed that, too," mumbled Jefferson. "But we're no closer now than we were at daybreak."

By that time Patrick could hardly breathe, much less talk. All he could do was paddle, and his arms felt disconnected from the rest of his body. Paddle, rest. Paddle, rest.

"There must be an offshore current," continued Jefferson.

As far as Patrick could tell, they were moving sideways, but he couldn't spare the words to answer Jefferson until he saw a dark shape move in the clear water just ahead of them.

"Another shark!" cried Patrick. Almost by instinct he yanked up his legs as he had the night before, curling up into a tight ball.

Jefferson shouted and slapped at the water, then paused and watched. A dark bullet shape darted underneath them. Patrick felt the power of something swimming just below his feet. "See any fins?" asked Jefferson, but Patrick could not. He wanted to close his eyes in the terror of the moment. Something breathed out a puff of air just behind his head.

"What's that?" he cried, whirling around to face his attacker. Instead, he saw a pair of jet black eyes set in the face of what looked like a large dog. He could have reached out and touched the animal, which was joined by another, then another.

"We have some company," laughed Jefferson, holding out a hand. "Seals."

Patrick relaxed and unfolded his legs back into the water. But it still hurt to smile, so he just stared back at the curious animals. At one time he counted at least fifteen or twenty bobbing around them.

"Too bad we can't talk them into towing us in," said Jefferson. "I think we're being pushed out to sea again."

But just as quickly as they had arrived, the curious seals ducked back under the waves. A moment later Patrick caught sight of them nearer to the shore, leaping and flying through the water.

"Did I say something wrong?" Jefferson called out. "Come back here!"

Patrick just sighed and commanded his aching arms to start paddling once more. He had long since kicked off his shoes. Somehow he got his legs moving again, too.

"I can't keep this up much longer," Patrick finally whispered, not loud enough for Jefferson to hear.

"I think it's getting closer!" Jefferson reported their progress.

Patrick rested his cheek on the mangled life ring and kicked, not knowing where the strength came from. The lighthouse had long since disappeared from view.

We're going to make it, he imagined, but then his eyes focused on something else in the water. Something circling closer and closer.

"Keep swimming," ordered Jefferson, and Patrick obeyed, knowing they were swimming closer to a half-dozen shark fins.

So many, Patrick thought as they desperately paddled on. *What happened to the seals?*

"If we make it through this," grunted Jefferson, "I promise you I'll help you find your pa."

Patrick nodded and closed his eyes again, shaking and certain at the same time. "Out of the way, sharks," he breathed. "We haven't come this far without help." *Please, God*.

With each kick he felt more and more sure of what he was doing. Patrick snapped open his eyes. The fins were still circling while Jefferson paddled steadily.

"Ha!" Patrick cried and slapped the water with his free hand. He knew he had no strength left, but somehow his arms and legs kept moving.

Jefferson looked at Patrick as if he were crazy, then picked up the act.

"Ha!" cried Jefferson, slapping at the water on his side of the life ring. "Ha!"

Something rough brushed against Patrick's leg—the same sandpaper roughness he had felt the night before. But instead of drawing back, this time Patrick kicked as hard as he could. He missed and lost his grip on the life ring, slipping underwater, suspended only by the rope still tied around his wrist. He was certain that the large, blurry shape in front of his face was not a friendly fur seal.

"Ha!" Patrick cried out underwater, and he thrashed out with his fist. Somehow he made contact with the snout of a shark twice his size. The powerful animal squirmed away, and Patrick burst from the water, still shouting and slapping.

"Hold on!" cried Jefferson, pointing to the breakers just ahead.

Patrick grabbed at the life ring as a wave picked them up. They surged toward the crash of surf, tumbling in the wave's foam. The rope yanked painfully at the raw skin of his wrist. He tried to hold his breath underwater, and for what seemed forever he wasn't even sure which way was up, or which way to swim for air. Jefferson's elbow or knee—he couldn't tell which—connected with his stomach, and they spun together in a tangled mess. Patrick could hold his breath no longer, and everything went black.

CHAPTER 13

SOMEONE IS WATCHING US

Patrick woke coughing, his face in the dirt. It hurt to lift his chin. Everything still felt as if it were rocking from side to side, so he wasn't quite sure if he was really on dry land.

"Jefferson?" He tried to talk, but his throat was almost parched shut, and the only thing that escaped from his mouth was a weak squawk.

When he could focus his eyes, which he could do only with a mighty effort, he saw that Jefferson Pitney was next to him on the dry ground. Dead, maybe.

"Jefferson?" he reached over and shook the other boy by the shoulder. Jefferson did not move.

Patrick rubbed his raw wrist, but the rope was mysteriously gone. Somehow they had crawled or been dragged up a narrow beach at the mouth of a steep, wooded canyon. Out of reach of the waves, he found himself in a crazy tangle of tents, ropes, and harpoons: the remains of what had once been a camp of some kind. Behind him lay the small, sheltered cove where they had washed up onto shore. It shone emerald blue in the bright sunshine and was ringed by jagged boulders. Above them on both sides towered the hazy cliffs Patrick had seen from the ocean.

"Jefferson, wake up." Patrick managed to find his voice as he shook Jefferson's shoulder again. "We've been asleep for . . ."

For how long? Patrick had no way of knowing. The shadows cast by the scrub bush around him told him it was late afternoon or early morning. Afternoon, probably. But what day was it? He had lost track.

Jefferson groaned. The older boy lashed out with his arm, grazing Patrick's ear.

"No, stay away," moaned Jefferson, swinging his arms again as if he were swimming. "Stay away! You can't touch me! Ha! Get away!"

Patrick rolled Jefferson onto his back and held down his arms. "It's all right," he told him hoarsely. "Wake up."

Jefferson's eyelids rolled open, and he looked in terror at Patrick before he calmed down. Sand covered his face like a beard.

"Oh," said Jefferson. He brushed off his face and coughed. "You're a horrible sight to wake up to. Am I alive?"

"What do you think?" Patrick rolled over onto his back and stared up at the sky. His arms and legs still throbbed with pain.

"You sure you're alive?" Jefferson sat up slowly and looked into Patrick's face. "You're all red and puffy. And your lips look like overcooked sausages."

"Thanks." Patrick tried to stand but stumbled on his first step. It took both of them leaning on the other for them to stand.

"I don't know how we got here." Jefferson looked around. "I remember something about someone grabbing me, and I tried to fight. Then nothing."

Patrick pointed to the twin sets of lines where their heels had been dragged through the beach sand and then through the dirt to the middle of the camp. "Looks as if someone pulled us up from the water. You remember more than I do."

"Hmm," said Jefferson. "Seal hunters' camp, I expect. Or at least it used to be."

"Looks deserted, all right," Patrick agreed.

Jefferson shook his head and picked up a clay jug with a cork plug. "Well, look at this," he said, uncorking the jug and sniffing it carefully. "Smells like fresh water!"

When it was Patrick's turn, he drank until his stomach was

awash with the stale but wonderful water. Satisfied, they searched the camp more carefully. Three lean-to tents were in shreds, clustered around a central fire pit full of cold ashes and fish bones. An ax with a broken handle was parked in a log stump next to the pit.

"Food!" cried Patrick, unwrapping a bundle of leaves that someone had placed on the ground at the edge of the camp. He wasn't sure what kind of meat it was, but it tasted salty, gamey, and not unpleasant.

"Reminds me of venison," said Jefferson between hungry mouthfuls.

"I wouldn't know." Patrick looked around the mess. "It looks as if someone put this food where we would see it when we woke up."

They could both see footprints in the dirt of the camp and around the fire pit. Patrick followed one set of tracks down to the water's edge, where Jefferson joined him. They stood still to watch a flock of large birds come winging around the point.

"Everything's different about this place," said Patrick, staring at the lopsided birds, as big as eagles but with enormous beaks that hung down in mighty pouches. The birds flew single file out across the ocean, nearly dragging the waves.

"You've never seen a pelican before?" Jefferson put his hands on his hips.

"I guess I haven't seen a lot of things. This *is* Australia, though, isn't it? But where is everyone?"

"Could be an island. I'm not sure. First thing we have to do is reach that lighthouse we saw down the coast." Jefferson looked down at his bare feet and frowned. "Problem is, I don't think I can climb up that steep ravine barefoot. It looks rough."

Patrick nodded. He was still wobbly on his feet, and his face blazed as if it had just come out of the fire. At least his throat was feeling better after the water and the meat. But where would they get more food? He worried as they returned to the camp to survey what they had.

Jefferson held up a native spear of a carved wood as hard as iron,

101

with a primitive but menacing barb. "Two harpoons," he counted, "these ripped-up old clothes—"

"And two old pairs of boots!" Patrick held up the shoes in triumph.

Jefferson inspected a hole in the toe. "Better than going barefoot, I suppose."

Patrick heard a rustle from somewhere in the bushes behind him, and he was sure it was more than just the wind from the cove. "Did you hear that?" He whirled around but couldn't see anything.

"Probably a kangaroo."

Patrick shook his head. "That was no kangaroo. Someone's watching us."

"I doubt that." Jefferson took another bite of meat. "There's nobody around for miles."

But Patrick wasn't convinced. "Well, then, how were we dragged out of the water? And what about these other footprints here at the camp?"

"They were probably here before. You've been reading too much *Robinson Crusoe*. Remember the book where the fellow gets washed up on a desert island and spots the footprints? My father read that to me before he—"

"I've never read that book," Patrick interrupted quietly, reminded of his own family again. He sank to his knees in the sandy dirt and looked out at the setting sun over the golden ocean. He searched desperately for a sail on the horizon.

Lord, where am I? he asked silently, head in his hands. *Ma and everyone on the ship think I'm dead. Becky's probably trying to help Ma. Michael won't understand why this happened, especially not after losing Pa, too. And now . . .*

"Don't worry, kid," Jefferson told him, resting a hand on Patrick's shoulder. Patrick jumped at the unexpected touch. "We'll head for the lighthouse first thing tomorrow."

The lighthouse. It had to be miles away. In the meantime, he could almost feel the watching eyes from the bushes, and it made him shiver.

CHAPTER 14

LIKE ROBINSON CRUSOE

The next morning Patrick awoke sitting up. His empty stomach ached, and his eyes were wet with tears. He rubbed his eyes, trying to remember where he was.

"What were you dreaming about over there?" Jefferson was pulling on his boots as he sat on the ground not far away. "You've been whimpering like a puppy dog all night."

Patrick's only answer was the growling of his empty stomach. He jumped up, pulled on his own boots, and walked over to the hunters' harpoons.

"What are you going to do with that thing?" Jefferson stood up slowly.

"I'm going fishing." Patrick wrinkled his nose and took a deep breath of the tangy salt air. "Aren't you hungry?"

"Sure. But we're going to eat it raw?"

"I'll catch the fish. You start the fire."

Jefferson stood with his hands on his hips and stared down at the cold charcoal of the fire pit. "Listen, Patrick, I'm a farmer's boy from Arkansas, not a magician. Do *you* know how to make a fire out here?"

"I thought you could try turning a stick between your hands or something."

"Fine, I'll give it a try. You just get us something to eat."

"Better hurry," Patrick called back over his shoulder. "I'll only be a few minutes."

"Huh," Jefferson grunted back.

Patrick jogged down to the sandy beach and took up a station beside a pair of rocks where the waves crashed and water collected in a series of rocky pools. He stood still for a few minutes, his arm raised with the sealer's sharp metal harpoon.

"Here, fishy, fishy."

Below his feet he could see a few small fish, too small to catch, and a lot of greenish, waving kelp, like seaweed. The pool, which was open to the sea at one end, was just big enough so that Patrick couldn't jump across. Finally a curious pink fish peeked its head out from behind the kelp.

"Aha," yelled Patrick, casting the hefty spear into the water with all his strength. "Breakfast!"

The harpoon sliced cleanly into the green water, but the fish had disappeared even before Patrick let go of his spear.

"It's a wee bit deeper than I thought," he murmured, wading gingerly into the tide pool to retrieve the spear. A jellyfish squirted under his heel, and he slid backward into the water, which came up to his chest.

"Whoa!" he cried, standing up in the pool. "Not at all what I had in mind."

Searching with his toe, he located the harpoon and lifted it back up for another try.

"This time you're not getting away," he warned the fish as he stood dripping at the edge of the pool.

An hour later his clothes were still wet from falling in two more times. He looked back toward the camp, hoping Jefferson was having a better time of it. No smoke. He sighed.

"Maybe Jefferson can give it a try," Patrick grumbled. His boots made wet, squishing noises as he trudged up the trail, and for a moment he thought he heard something—or someone—rustling in the bushes behind him.

"Jefferson?" Patrick stopped to listen but heard nothing, so he continued up the trail.

Jefferson didn't look up from his pile of dried grass and twigs as Patrick came to stand beside him.

"So how many fish did you catch?" he asked, blowing at the grass. Patrick couldn't see so much as a hint of a spark. "I've almost got it going."

"I guess I'm as good a fisherman as you are a fire starter," Patrick answered quietly.

Jefferson fanned the grass some more, then knocked two rocks together. Finally he threw the rocks down in disgust.

"Ah, it's no use," he fumed. "Well, we can't just sit here and wait for more food to drop out of the sky. The only thing to do is head up the coast before we starve to death."

Patrick wasn't so sure.

"The lighthouse," Jefferson reminded him. "There has to be someone living there."

"Of course." Patrick pulled a musty smock over his head. It smelled like campfires and seaweed, and it was horribly itchy, but at least it was dry.

Jefferson gathered up his nearly empty water jug and started climbing up the ravine. "Come on, Robinson Crusoe!" he called back. "We can't stay here."

Patrick looked around one last time at the camp and sighed, but he knew Jefferson was right. They would have to find help soon—or starve.

Patrick kept an eye behind them as they climbed, half expecting to see someone lurking in the bushes, following them.

"What do the natives around here look like?" he asked Jefferson as they made their way up the steep ravine.

"You don't know anything, do you?" Jefferson paused to wipe his brow. "I hear they're dark as night, just like the slaves back home in America. Don't you all have slaves in Ireland?"

Patrick shook his head, puzzled. "No, and I thought—"

"I know what you thought." Jefferson's voice suddenly turned sharp. "Lincoln freed the slaves. The war between the states is over, and I should be shaking the Northerners' hands howdy-do. Fact is, the Yankees killed my pa, and you can't tell me . . ." Jefferson's voice trailed off. They weren't talking about natives and slaves anymore.

"I'm sorry," Patrick's voice was quiet. "You never told me about your family before."

"You never told me about *your* pa, either. Not at first." Jefferson stared hard into the bush and kept climbing.

"You father was killed in the war?" Patrick decided to take a chance with another question.

" 'Course, we didn't have any slaves, but did the Yankees believe us? No."

"Which Yankees?" Patrick wasn't quite following what Jefferson was saying.

Jefferson leaned against a rock and turned to face Patrick, his nostrils puffing like a bull's. "Just Yankees. They killed my father, who never did anything to anybody. He was just a one-legged farmer from Arkansas. And they killed him 'cause he was in their way."

Patrick didn't dare interrupt as Jefferson drew in a deep, jagged breath.

"I was twelve," continued Jefferson. "I saw them when they came for him. I saw it all."

The tears in Jefferson's eyes overflowed, and he turned away before he broke down completely. Patrick put his arm around Jefferson's shoulder, the same way the older boy had done with him the night before.

"I'm sorry," Patrick whispered as Jefferson's tears puddled the dusty ground at their feet. "I'm sorry." It didn't seem nearly enough, but it was all he could think of to say.

Jefferson took another breath, shook off Patrick's arm, and looked him straight in the eye. "There, now I've told you, and that's the only telling I'm going to do. You see now why I have to help you find *your* pa?"

Patrick nodded. There was still something else he had to know. "If you don't mind, what about your mother?"

"She died when I was born," Jefferson answered without further emotion. "I never knew her. You're lucky you have a mother."

"Lucky?" Patrick's thoughts turned back to his mother and Becky and Michael. "Everyone thinks I'm dead."

"So let's find out where we are." Jefferson sniffed. "Maybe we can change that."

As they tripped up the steep, rough trail, Patrick looked at his traveling companion in a new way. But he still couldn't stop thinking about his own family, wondering where they were and what they were doing. They kept climbing in silence.

"Come on!" Jefferson finally urged him from the ridge at the top. His hair stood on end in the stiff breeze. "You can see almost everything from up here."

It had taken them all morning, but at last they were standing on the top of the cliff. Behind them stretched miles of wooded hills. Below, the sea twinkled in the sunlight. Even higher, hills blocked their view to the right.

"This is Australia?" asked Patrick, his hands on his knees. He still didn't feel very good, and his skin felt sunburned and raw. Jefferson didn't look much better, but he seemed to ignore it.

"Could be," Jefferson said. "But I think we may be on an island off the coast."

"It's a big island if it is. What do we do now?"

Jefferson stood still for a minute, as if sniffing a distant wind, then he took a long drink from the jug of water he had tied over his shoulder.

"We keep heading toward the lighthouse."

As they continued walking, they could see a eucalyptus forest in the distance, covered by a light blue haze. Between them and the forest stretched a hilly plain. Several tall shapes moving along the edge of the forest caught Patrick's eye.

"There," he pointed excitedly. "I think I see someone!"

Jefferson squinted into the distance as they walked. "Your brother should be here to see this. It's a bunch of kangaroos."

Patrick wasn't quite sure whether to believe Jefferson; the figures in the distance looked almost like men. But when the rusty red shapes started hopping away, there was no mistake.

"I've never seen anything like that," whistled Patrick, standing still. A half dozen other smaller kangaroos followed the larger animals, and soon they disappeared out of view.

"You'll see plenty more." Jefferson bent down to adjust the old leather straps on his boots and wiggled the toe that stuck out in front. "I think I know where we are now."

"You do?"

Jefferson nodded. "We were headed for Adelaide when the gale hit us from behind." He pointed behind them and waved his hand to illustrate. "If we were pushed toward the coast this way, we could have washed up on a place called Kangaroo Island. Biggest island off the coast in these parts."

"So where are all the people?" asked Patrick, stopping to rest. "Doesn't anyone live here?" He shaded his eyes against the bright sun of early afternoon.

Jefferson shrugged and kept walking. "Maybe they're at the lighthouse." He plucked a handful of blue-green leaves as he walked by a eucalyptus tree, and Patrick's stomach rumbled.

Don't think about food, Patrick told himself. He picked one of the leaves and rubbed it between his hands. The heady, almost minty fragrance of eucalyptus oil scented the air. Still, they kept walking, up hills, through dense bushes, down more hills, through more dense bushes. At one point Patrick suspected they were going in circles, and his mind wandered. A huge lizard, as big as his arm, flashed away under his foot.

"Did you see that thing?" A shiver went up Patrick's spine, and he jumped backward as the reptile slithered away into the bushes. "It looked like a dragon!"

Jefferson didn't answer; he was too far ahead. There was nothing to do but catch up.

"Slow down, Jeff!" Patrick called out. The afternoon was turning into evening, and he was growing sore and tired. "Do you even know where we are?"

Patrick's legs seemed as if they would no longer carry him. Below and to the left he could barely hear the crashing surf against the coastal cliffs. Above and ahead he could see the first star of the evening.

"You want another drink?" asked Jefferson, now only a few steps ahead.

"Please," answered Patrick. "I can't keep going."

He pushed the branches out of his face as they swung back to hit him. Some particularly thorny bushes snagged at his legs, and he was glad for the huge dungarees—heavy cotton pants—he had found at the camp.

"We should have run into the lighthouse a long time ago." Jefferson sounded sure of himself. "I think the trail's back up this way."

As they continued through the scrub, Patrick felt the ground shift.

Strange, he thought, and he stopped to catch his breath. He hopped up and down, and the earth bounced back like a sponge, except it wasn't wet.

"Jefferson!" Patrick took a couple of steps and yelled into the darkness ahead of him. "Stop for a minute."

"I'm right here," said the other boy. They nearly collided as Jefferson jumped up and down just as Patrick had done.

"This is really odd, Patrick," said Jefferson, still bouncing. "Do you feel—"

But Jefferson never got to finish his sentence as the earth beneath them collapsed. They tumbled straight down. It was almost as if Patrick were back in the waves, captured by the surf. Only instead of salt water, he was surrounded by dust, sod, and bushes as he and Jefferson tumbled in a terrifying, earthy avalanche.

There was no use screaming in the darkness. For a moment Patrick had no idea of up or down, sideways or backward. They had just been swallowed alive, and it had all happened so fast. If not for Jefferson's head parked painfully in his side, he wouldn't have known if he were alive or dead.

"What happened?" Patrick tried to ask, but the darkness only sucked the words from his mouth. More dirt cascaded on top of him, like a waterfall that couldn't be stopped, and he felt his left arm pinned behind him. A moment later something told him he was now upside down—maybe it was the blood pounding in his head.

Jefferson wiggled and groaned in pain.

"Jefferson!" Patrick reached out with his free right arm and managed to grab hold of the other boy's hair. "Jefferson, are you all right?"

"Huh?" Jefferson puffed and wheezed, sounding confused and pained. "Where are you?"

"Right here beside you," answered Patrick. He tried to move, to get Jefferson's head out of his side, but something had wedged him tightly in position. He pushed and the earth gave way once more. They slid and rolled down the side of a mound of dirt.

"Ahh!" Jefferson yelped.

Patrick touched Jefferson's arm in the darkness. "Are you hurt?" He knew the answer to his question before he asked it.

"My leg . . . oh, it got twisted behind me."

They were still for a moment as the earthquake—or whatever it had been—settled down. Patrick shook his head to clear the dirt from his ears, and he heard water dripping, echoing far off to the sides. Unlike the hot, dry air above, it was suddenly cool and damp. He looked up. The evening star he had seen as they walked was suddenly much higher overhead, visible through a dark, jagged window of a hole.

Patrick cleared his throat. "I think we fell down into some kind of cave."

CHAPTER 15

SWALLOWED

"Now we've really done it," croaked Jefferson. "We've stepped on a sinkhole."

"It wasn't your fault," Patrick tried to reassure him as he felt his way around the dark chamber. By the light of the moon, he could barely make out eerie shapes all around them, what looked like huge, shiny icicles made of rock hanging from the ceiling around the opening of the hole. Here and there, upside-down rock icicles rose up from the floor to meet the ones from the ceiling, and they glowed silver in the early evening. But that was all he could see, even as his eyes adjusted to the darkness.

"Have you ever been in a cave before?" asked Patrick.

"Not like this. And I'd just as soon not—oww . . ."

"Can you stand?" Patrick tried to help Jefferson up, but the other boy was heavier than he thought.

"I . . . I think so. My leg was only twisted. It isn't broken."

"You're sure?"

"Almost sure. It just smarts." But Jefferson didn't sound so sure.

"Then I'm going to see if there's any way up." Patrick tested a wall, but it was as slick as the wall of the tide pool where he had fallen earlier. He pulled his hand back with a groan.

"It's all slimy," he told Jefferson. "There's no way we're going to get up that wall. I'd guess we're about fifteen feet down."

"Hello!" Jefferson yelled into the cave without warning, and Patrick jumped as the echo pulsed through the darkness before slowly dying.

"Sounds big," reported Jefferson. He stooped and threw something into the black, and Patrick heard the clatter of a rock disappear with an echo into a deep hole to their right. "It looks like the ground just opened up and swallowed us. Kind of like a story out of your Bible."

Patrick could barely see Jefferson's outline, now standing next to him. They stayed still for several minutes, staring up at the stars through the gaping hole in the cave's ceiling.

"I didn't know you knew any Bible stories, Jefferson."

"I went to Sunday school, same as everyone else back home. My aunt dragged me along till I was old enough to run away Sunday mornings. Then me and some of my friends would slip out and go fishing down at the river. It just didn't stick with me, all that Jesus talk."

Patrick could hear the quiet but steady *drip, drip* of the cave around them. He was afraid to peer more closely at the darkness, afraid of what he might see. He shivered in the dampness while Jefferson kept talking.

"But I remember old Miz Hendricks telling us the Lord was going to smite us the same way He did—what was his name—Korah? The fellow with Moses who the ground opened up and swallowed? She said we were going to hell just like Korah if we ran away from her Sunday school."

Jefferson imitated the voice of his teacher. " 'If you boys don't listen,' she used to yell at us, 'y'all will be joining Korah in evahlastin' darkness!' "

The cave was quiet for a moment until Jefferson continued. "Now look at where I am." Jefferson's words echoed through the chambers around them.

Patrick wished he could say something wise, but he couldn't stop shivering or keep his teeth from chattering.

"Now, if it was just me who was swallowed up," Jefferson went on, "maybe I'd start to think old Miz Hendricks was right. But here you are in the hole with me even though you're religious. So whatever it is we're down here for, we're both guilty."

Patrick stooped and held his head, trying to stop the shivering.

"I-it's n-not for anything we d-d-did," Patrick managed to say. "But maybe God is trying to get our attention."

"I suppose He's done that." Jefferson sounded too cheerful, as if he were trying to make up by his tone of voice for the fact that they were lost on a strange island and now trapped in a dark cave. "But just the same, I think we better hunker down here for the night and wait for some light."

"Y-yes," agreed Patrick. He wasn't about to move into the darkness where the hole was, so he crouched back down, hugged his legs, held on to his grandmother's ring, and prayed. Once in a while he would drift away into a dreamless sleep, but he would wake right back up, shivering and afraid of falling into the pit so close by.

Sometime during the long night he remembered a Bible verse his father had read to their family several times years ago. Now the words came back to him, and they seemed to have been written exactly for this time.

"If I make my bed in the deep," he whispered the words as best he could remember them, "even then, you are there. Even if I settle on the far side of the sea, you're there, too. Darkness is like daylight to you."

"Hmph," muttered Jefferson. "Darkness looks just like darkness to me."

Patrick lost count of the number of times he woke during the long night, but he got the feeling that he was awake more than he was asleep. Always cramped, always cold, always damp, always shivering. He thought about the pit where Jefferson had thrown the stone.

How deep is it? he worried quietly. *And are we alone?*

He listened for sounds, for bats, for anything that might be crawling around down there with them. And he tried to keep the shadows from turning into tall black creatures, the same kind of creatures that used to hide in the shadows of his room when he was little and trying to get to sleep. All he could hear was Jefferson's slow breathing and the constant *drip, drip* of the cavern.

"Are you awake?" he finally asked, hoping Jefferson would answer. Nothing. "Guess not."

He recited the Bible verse again about God being there with him in the darkness, and it helped, but he still shivered as he waited for the dawn's light.

If I keep my eyes closed, he told himself, *I won't see the creatures in the shadows.*

The next thing he knew, Jefferson was standing over him, looking larger than life in the pink light filtering down from the hole. "Is it morning?" Patrick struggled to his feet. "I must have fallen asleep somehow."

"Watch it." Jefferson held on to his shoulder and pointed behind him. "Don't step that way."

Patrick looked back to see that they had been sleeping on the edge of a cliff—only two feet from falling in.

Jefferson peered into the dark hole and whistled. "Hoo-eey, looks as if we were pretty lucky last night, not rolling a few inches farther." Then he crossed his arms and grinned, his face looking like a coal miner's, covered in a mask of dust. " 'Course, that's not what you and old Miz Hendricks would say, is it?"

Patrick felt cold and hungry, stiff and sore, but it felt wonderful to be alive. And he knew exactly what had happened last night.

"God didn't stop us here on this ledge for no reason, Jeff." Patrick gathered up his courage and peeked over into the darkness. "You've got to be seeing that by now, haven't you?"

Jefferson didn't answer, just backed away from the edge and climbed over the pile of earth that had cascaded down with them last night. Even at the top of the pile, they were at least fifteen feet down into the cave. Far out of reach of escape.

"Well, we're still in this hole." He turned to Patrick at last. "Might as well be a grave."

If this is a grave, Patrick told himself, *it's the most beautiful one I've ever seen.*

The gathering sunlight filtered down from the hole, filling the cave with soft light. They were just inside a huge room, filled from floor to ceiling with the rock icicles that they had only barely seen in the starlight the night before.

"Look at these things," said Jefferson, climbing up to a giant set of icicles. "They're gigantic."

"How's your leg?" Patrick asked.

Jefferson responded by hopping up and down on one leg, then the other. "Smarts a little, but it's fine."

For the next hour they explored the cave, Patrick's empty stomach reminding him that they would have to find a way out soon. He wished he still had some of the dried meat from the camp, but he was more thirsty than anything else.

"Hey, over here!" Jefferson shouted, the echo making it hard to tell where he was.

"Where are you?" Patrick called back, trying not to stumble in the shadows.

"Over here . . . here," the voice echoed back. Patrick finally found Jefferson kneeling by the edge of a small stream.

"Best water I've tasted in a long time," Jefferson told him, cupping his hands and drinking the water hungrily. "Fill up your stomach, and you won't be so hungry."

Patrick followed the other boy's advice, first washing the dirt from his face and arms.

"You're right," Patrick answered, coming up for air. "It's sweet." *But we can't live on sweet water*, he wanted to add. As he kneeled by the water, his hand brushed against something cool and smooth.

"What's this?" he asked, picking up a small tin cup. It had been nestled in a shallow rock shelf next to the stream.

"Where'd you get that?" asked Jefferson.

Patrick turned the cup over in his hands. "Right here by the water. It's not rusty."

"Here, let me see." Jefferson took the cup and held it up to the dim light from the hole.

"This has to mean someone's been down here," Patrick concluded. "Which means—"

"Which means there has to be a way out besides the way we came in!"

Jefferson was right. There had to be another way in. Trouble was, they could make out four different tunnels opening into the main cavern where they stood. Each as dark as black ink.

"One of these tunnels leads out of here," said Jefferson. "All we have to do is choose the right one."

"Well . . ." Patrick tried to think. "We can't climb out of the hole—"

"True."

"And no one knows we're down here to rescue us."

"Right again."

"So we can't just sit here and drink water the rest of our lives."

"Which tunnel, though?" wondered Jefferson. "They're all dark."

Patrick looked back at the sunlight and tapped the tin cup in his palm. "Too bad our friend with the cup didn't leave us a rope."

"Or a ladder." Jefferson shivered.

"You're shivering." asked Patrick. "Why would you be shivering?"

"I don't know. It's just drafty, I suppose."

"That's right! It's drafty. Did you hear what you just said?"

"What are you talking about?"

"Don't you see?" Patrick sprang up and ran out to the place where they had spent the night. "This sinkhole opened up, and now it's drafty. So where's the draft coming from?"

"Ohh . . ."

"From another opening! So all we have to do is find out where the draft is coming from and we're out."

"Hey, you're not so bad," said Jefferson, "for an eleven-year-old."

"Twelve," Patrick corrected him. "I'm twelve."

Patrick skipped back to the place where the four tunnels opened into the main cavern.

"Can you feel a breeze coming in through any of them?" he asked.

They stood still in front of each tunnel, trying to feel a draft against their faces.

"Nothing here," reported Jefferson, and the second opening was the same.

"Here," cried Patrick. "I feel it!"

Jefferson stood in front of the last tunnel, licked his finger, and held it up quietly. "There's a draft coming out of this one, too."

"So maybe there are two ways out of here," guessed Patrick. "Which one?"

"I'd flip a coin if I had one," answered Jefferson. "You choose."

Patrick held his breath and stepped into the larger of the two tunnels. He looked back at the light, then back to the darkness. "I'll go first."

"No, I will."

At first the ceiling was high overhead. But only a few steps into the tunnel, Jefferson grunted in pain.

"Bumped my head," he warned. "And it feels as if the floor is rising up, too."

"Maybe we should have taken the other tunnel," admitted Patrick.

"As long as we don't run into any pits, let's move forward. I can still feel the air in my face."

So did Patrick, and it was the one thing that kept him going. He couldn't get used to the odd feeling of not knowing whether his eyes were open or shut. Either way, all he could see was pitch blackness.

"Sorry," Patrick apologized for the second time as he bumped into Jefferson from behind. "Seems as though we've been going in circles."

"We might as well be upside down and backward, for all I can tell."

"Wait." Patrick paused for a moment, trying to regain his sense of direction. "This tunnel isn't as straight as it seemed."

"That's for sure."

"And can you feel the air anymore?"

There was a moment of silence.

"I can't feel a thing," said Jefferson.

"That's what I was afraid of." Patrick sighed. "We probably made a wrong turn and didn't even realize there was one in the darkness."

"So we better turn around and go back."

"Exactly."

They turned around as best they could, and Jefferson took the lead again. He shuffled and complained each time he hit his head or stubbed his toe. After a half hour of stumbling, he stopped once more.

"We should be back to where we started by now," he whispered, and Patrick knew he was right.

"We're in some kind of maze," Patrick admitted.

Neither said anything for a few minutes, and they stood silently, each in his own thoughts.

"Maybe we should split up?" Jefferson finally suggested.

"Are you crazy?"

"No, just trying to think of what to do. This is not the way I wanted to—"

"Don't say that. We're going to get out of here."

"How? Are you just going to pray us out?"

Patrick didn't reply.

"I . . . I didn't mean it," Jefferson said after a minute or two of silence. "You can pray all you want. Couldn't hurt."

Frustrated with trying to see in the dark, Patrick kept his eyes closed and tried to imagine the maze where they were trapped. The sinkhole and the main cavern. The four tunnels, maybe connected. The two that led to another opening or openings. Which way to go now?

"Well, let's just keep going forward," suggested Patrick. "Maybe if we stay to the right, we'll come all the way around."

"It's better than sitting here and crying," Jefferson agreed.

They started off again, trying always to brush against the right side of the tunnel.

"Here's another cutoff," Jefferson reported when they quickly came to a dead end and had to turn around. The same thing happened two or three more times; Patrick lost count.

"How long do you figure we've been wandering around down here?" Jefferson finally asked.

"Three, maybe four hours," guessed Patrick, licking his lips. He turned his head to the side and felt something on his face.

"Hey," he whispered, and he licked his lips again. The feeling was the same. "I think I feel a breeze again."

"Good man!" Jefferson bubbled. Patrick could almost see the other boy's grin in the dark. "We're moving in the right direction again. Only this time we're not going to lose the scent!"

Picking up their steps, they followed the feeling of the breeze, careful not to lose it in the twists and turns of the tunnel.

"Still got it?" Patrick asked.

"Straight ahead, partner."

Patrick's eyes by then were playing tricks on him; sometimes he saw bright stars or twinkling red streaks, like fireworks. He was tempted to rub his eyes just to see the fireworks. But then something else caught his eye.

"It's getting lighter up ahead," announced Jefferson. "This is the way."

Feeling as if he were a bloodhound hot on the trail, Patrick held on to the back of Jefferson's shirt and tried not to trip the other boy. His eyes drank in the light—still dim, but growing stronger with every step.

"Ow!" cried Jefferson, ducking down for a low ceiling. Patrick did the same. Suddenly they were out of the tunnel and in a large, echoing cavern filled with the sound of running and dripping water.

Jefferson stopped in his tracks.

"Do you see it?" Patrick asked him. "Do you see the way out?"

"I see it." But Jefferson's voice told Patrick that something was wrong. He stepped around the older boy to see for himself.

"Oh," whispered Patrick. "Well, at least we're not lost anymore."

"Right back where we started."

They both sighed and sat down on the cold rock floor near where they had spent the night. Looking up into the blue sky above felt good after spending so many hours in the dark. *If only it weren't so far away. . . .*

"Hey!" Without warning, Jefferson put his head back and shouted into the sky. "Help! Hey!"

Patrick didn't have the energy to join him, and he knew it wouldn't help to remind Jefferson that no one was up there to hear.

"Doesn't anybody care that we're down here?" complained Jefferson. He stood up and paced around the bottom of the hole as Patrick had done earlier, trying the slippery wall for a foothold.

Patrick sat listening to the dripping inside the cave and straining his ears for any sounds that would come from above. Birds, animals, the wind, anything. But all he heard was the dripping and Jefferson's pacing—and then something else at the far side of the cave, near the entrance to the tunnels. The hair on the back of Patrick's neck stood on end when he again heard the sound of footsteps. He backed away slowly, his heart racing.

"Ahem."

Someone was clearing his throat.

Patrick grabbed Jefferson's knee as he walked by. He pointed at a flickering light emerging from the darkness.

"Jeff, look!"

"What—" Jefferson began. They both stood.

"You boys looking for a way out of this cavern?" came a soft, nasal Australian voice. All Patrick could see was the flickering light and a shadowy outline.

"Who are you?" Jefferson challenged the voice.

Patrick felt as stiff as a fencepost.

"Name's Luke," the stranger said, moving closer. As Luke neared, Patrick realized their rescuer wasn't any older than they were. Thirteen or fourteen at most, with wild black hair and skin almost as dark as the cave itself. He had on a worn pair of black trousers, ripped along the cuffs, and nothing else.

"Are you an aborigine?" Patrick asked slowly. "But you speak English." He had never seen anyone so dark, except in pictures.

The boy shifted his bottle torch from one hand to the other, his dark brown eyes sparkling in the flickering light when he laughed. "My, you're a real Pom, aren't you?"

"What's that?" Patrick took a step back in surprise.

"Pom—a red-cheeked Englishman."

"Oh. Well, I'm Irish, not English."

"I can hear that." The boy seemed to speak flawless English. "Who's your friend? Does he talk or just holler?"

"I'm Jefferson." The older boy kept his arms crossed and his square jaw set as he studied Luke. "Jefferson Paul Pitney."

"And you're American, aren't you?"

Patrick almost had to smile at the way this aborigine boy could speak perfect English and pick up on accents, like Jefferson's southern drawl.

"Arkansas," Jefferson replied through tight lips.

Luke grinned. "Arkansas. Little Rock."

Jefferson's jaw dropped open. "How do you know our state capital?"

The grin never left their rescuer's face. "Some sailors taught me capitals. Yankees. I talk to them whenever they visit. But most of them are friendlier than you two. Let's see . . . Massachusetts, Boston. Virginia, Richville—"

"That's Richmond," Jefferson corrected him.

"Of course." Luke smiled even more broadly. "Richmond." He turned with his smoldering homemade torch and made his way down the same tunnel they had tried just hours before.

"Where are we going?" Jefferson asked.

Luke paused for a moment but didn't turn around. "I thought you might want to get out of here, perhaps?"

Jefferson didn't answer and Luke continued. "A fellow on a

horse fell through a sinkhole into a cave just like you two a couple of years ago."

"What happened to him?" Patrick asked as he tried to catch up with the light.

"Died. You're lucky I was around to help you get out."

Patrick choked. "Well, we're very grateful."

"So you liked the 'roo, eh?"

"Did you say 'roo?"

"Salted kangaroo meat. You ate it all, didn't you?"

Patrick swallowed hard. "Quite good, yes, thank you. But why didn't you . . . why have you been hiding from us all this time?"

The boy shrugged. "Gates tells us that if strangers come, we should take care of them. He's never told us to meet them. Then you got yourself lost in this cave, and I figured you needed some help."

"So how did you—" Patrick wanted to ask him so many questions, but maybe now wasn't the time. Who was Gates, and what was this boy really up to?

"Here, hold this," Luke interrupted, holding out the torch for Patrick to take. "You have to get down on your belly and slither through this hole. I don't know if your friend here is going to fit."

"What hole?" Patrick peered into the shadows as Luke seemed to disappear into the floor.

"Where did he go?" wondered Jefferson, looking over Patrick's shoulder.

"I don't know. One minute—hey!"

Luke's grin broke through the darkness as he popped his head back out from a tiny opening behind a rock. "Are you coming?"

"We're right behind you." Patrick inspected the opening. It didn't look very promising.

"We're going through *that*?" Jefferson clearly couldn't believe it.

"It's the only way," answered Luke, reaching out his hand. "Hand me back the torch."

After Luke disappeared again, Patrick somehow managed to wiggle his feet, then his legs and shoulders, through the hole. He felt Luke's hands on his ankles, guiding him to a ledge. A minute later they were all standing together in another passageway, this one sloping up toward daylight.

"Next time you come walking by here, watch for sinkholes," Luke suggested as they finally stepped out into the sunlight. He blew out his bottle torch and hid it behind a rock before starting off down a trail.

"We will." Patrick had to stop and blink his eyes in the glowing afternoon sun. Everything was brighter than life, from the golden hills to the clear blue sky. He breathed in the air as if for the first time.

"Well, we made it." Jefferson grinned from ear to ear and shook Patrick's hand. "Didn't I tell you there was nothing to worry about? I knew where we were going the whole time."

Patrick stretched his arms toward the sky and laughed. "Is that a fact? That's not the way I remember it."

For a second Jefferson looked hurt, but then he grinned sheepishly. "Well . . ."

"As a matter of fact, you were awfully worried down there. If it weren't for me—" Patrick stopped in panic when he noticed their rescuer had disappeared. "He's gone!"

CHAPTER 16

GATES

"Aw, we don't need Luke," Jefferson began.

"Speak for yourself," said Patrick, running up a narrow trail that wandered over the open, golden hillside in the direction of the sea. He guessed they couldn't be far from the spot where they had fallen into the cave the day before.

"Patrick, don't get so excited," said Jefferson, but Patrick wasn't waiting.

"Luke!" he shouted. No reply. He sprinted to the crest of the hill and looked down toward the ocean. Luke was just stepping around another bend in the trail. "There you are. Luke!"

By the time Patrick caught up with the boy, he and Jefferson both were panting in the heat, and the breeze from the ocean felt good.

"We . . . thought we lost you again." Patrick gasped.

"Again?" Luke kept walking, only looked back in surprise. "I didn't know you lost me a first time."

They followed Luke along the cliffs as he half walked, half jogged the winding trail. Patrick thought the path seemed more suited to mountain goats, but he was happy that someone at least knew where they were going. Far below, he could see long rows of ocean breakers ending with a watery crash on a narrow strip of rocky beach. A pleasant, salty haze drifted up and flavored the air, already alive with the scent of blue-leaved eucalyptus. *If I weren't so hungry and thirsty*, thought Patrick, *I'd like to stay here awhile.*

"Where is he taking us?" Jefferson finally asked, and Patrick wondered why Jeff didn't ask Luke directly.

Luke didn't seem to mind. "Tell him we're going to see Gates," he answered without turning around. "He should be back from the mainland soon. He'll know what to do with you."

"Who's Gates?" asked Patrick as they rounded another bend in the trail.

As if in answer, Luke pointed to a stubby, square tower in the distance up ahead, commanding a barren but beautiful cliff set back a ways from the ocean. The lighthouse.

Patrick stopped to gawk for a moment.

"Who's Gates?" huffed Jefferson, a few steps behind Patrick. "Is he your master?"

Luke looked back at them with puzzled eyes.

"Patrick, tell your friend this is Kangaroo Island," he said at last, choosing his words carefully, "not Arkansas."

"Don't mind him," Patrick apologized, glaring at Jefferson. "He doesn't know any better. Not yet."

"So this really *is* Kangaroo Island." Jefferson sounded as if he knew it all along.

Luke nodded slightly and pointed up ahead. "And that's Cape Borda. Gates says—"

"Gates again," Jefferson interrupted, and Patrick winced at the older boy's rudeness. "You still haven't told us who this Gates fellow is."

"You'll find out."

"Why, you uppity—" complained Jefferson, but Patrick turned and stopped him before they took another step.

"You may be older, but it doesn't mean you can talk to people that way."

Jefferson stared at Patrick in surprise, but Patrick wasn't finished.

"This fellow drags us out of the ocean, feeds us, then rescues us from a cave, and all you can call him is 'uppity.' What's wrong with you?"

Still fuming, Patrick hurried after Luke.

If this is the way he's going to act, I don't care if he . . . if he
. . . Patrick wasn't sure how to finish the thought. He just wanted
to make sure he didn't lose Luke again, and he didn't really care if
Jefferson Paul Pitney followed them or not.

"Hold on, I'm coming," Jefferson called quietly. "Don't get upset."

But Patrick didn't slow down. Luke led them through another
stand of eucalyptus trees, through a brush-covered gully, and finally to a level, protected clearing just below the lighthouse. The
clearing was large enough to shelter a pair of trim stone cottages,
roofed with neat rows of hand-split wood shingles. An aborigine
woman squatted next to a small fire in the gravel courtyard in between. She hardly looked up as they approached, but two dogs that
looked like wild coyotes ran up to them with teeth bared and the
hair on their necks bristling.

"Hey, call off your dogs!" Jefferson stood back.

Luke only leaned against one of the cottages and grinned.

"I said, call off your dogs!" Jefferson put out his hands, but the
animals stood their ground.

Patrick had to laugh at the game Luke was playing. Finally Luke
gave an almost silent whistle, and the two dogs obediently turned
and trotted back toward their master.

Jefferson sighed with relief. "That's all we need," Jefferson said
to Patrick out of the side of his mouth. "We make it through the
sharks, only to have this kid's dogs chew us up on dry land."

"I think he's just trying to make a point," Patrick whispered
back.

"Whose side are you on?"

Luke pointed to one of the cottages. "Gates lives here."

"Why didn't you say so before?" Jefferson walked up to the front
door of the shack and knocked. No one answered. "Is Mrs. Gates
here?"

Luke nodded toward the edge of the clearing, where Patrick
could barely make out a plain wooden cross—a grave marker.

"Missus died when I was a little boy."

"I'm sorry," said Patrick quietly. He wasn't sure Luke heard him.

"But Gates should be back from the mainland maybe today, maybe tomorrow."

Jefferson frowned and stopped knocking. "He has a boat?"

"No, he swims," replied Luke, straight-faced.

Patrick covered his grin and patted one of the short-haired, biscuit-colored dogs on the head as it sniffed him eagerly. That was just the kind of teasing Jefferson usually gave others.

The woman still had said nothing as she stirred the pot of delicious-smelling stew. Maybe it was kangaroo meat again, but it was hard to tell. Of course, at that point just about anything would have smelled delicious to Patrick.

Jefferson looked hungrily at the stew—or whatever it was—and plunked down on a log next to the fire with a sigh.

"I'll wait here," he said.

"Suit yourself." Luke looked up for a brief second at Patrick. "Come here. I'll show you something."

Though tired and hungry, Patrick didn't mind following the other boy across the clearing, past the cottages, and up to the top of the bluff. Soon they were alone on the barren point. The faded, whitewashed lighthouse looked down at them.

"Want to see it?" asked Luke.

"Sure. I've never been in one before. But it's not very tall, is it?"

Luke led the way through a short door and up the winding staircase. "The hills are plenty tall enough already."

"Hmm."

"When I was little," Luke went on, "I used to think Gates kept the sun up here at night."

"Is Gates your father?" Patrick blurted out, instantly wishing he hadn't.

The boy laughed and held up the back side of his dark hand. "Does this look like English skin to you?" He shook his full crop of curly black hair. "English hair?"

Patrick took that as a no, but he still didn't quite understand Luke's relationship to Gates.

"So your parents . . ."

"My parents died when I was this big." Luke put his hand down close to the steps to show how tall a two- or three-year-old might stand.

"I'm sorry."

Patrick caught his breath as they stepped up to the open top platform. He stared at his reflection in the giant set of round glass lenses, larger than he could put his arms around, with the oil lantern in the middle and everything shining and polished.

"We're from over there." Luke pointed toward the distant mainland. "The Ngarrenderri tribe—my tribe—thought this was the place where the souls of the dead came to stay."

The thought sent a chill up Patrick's spine.

"But Bet, my mother's sister, she didn't believe that. She took care of me after my parents died, until Gates and Missus found us and took us back here to the island. They never had children of their own."

"And then Mrs. Gates died?"

Luke nodded seriously. "I remember her a little. She used to read me stories from the Bible. Now it's just Gates and me and my aunt Bet. She cooks. Takes care of things."

"Does she speak English?"

"My, you're full of questions." Luke smiled. "She understands some, but she doesn't like to speak it. But what about you?"

"Me?" Patrick wasn't sure he was as ready to tell his story, but the way Luke asked—as if he really wanted to know—made him feel comfortable.

"My friend and I fell off the *Star of Africa*—actually, Jefferson fell overboard during a storm, and I jumped to get a life ring to him. Now we have to get to Adelaide," continued Patrick, "to find my mother and sister and brother, who were on the ship with me."

"Gates goes to Adelaide sometimes. He can maybe take you there."

Patrick gripped the railing tightly. "Maybe? You don't understand. I *have* to get there right away. My family thinks I'm dead!"

Luke shrugged as he strolled around the light. "Better for them to think so than for it to be true."

"But . . ." Patrick protested. The other boy didn't stop walking. There was nothing to do but follow him in circles around the light.

"See down there?" Luke pointed at the ocean. "I get to fish any time I want. Back that way, where we came from, I explore the caves, like the one you fellows fell into."

"Who takes care of this lighthouse?" Patrick tapped the glass.

"Don't touch that. Gates, mostly. Sometimes he lets me help. Bet watches it when he's gone, but not too many people know that."

Patrick let the wind whip his hair as he leaned against the rail of the metal balcony. "Luke, thanks for pulling me and Jefferson out of the water the way you did."

Luke only grunted.

"And out of the cave." Patrick tried again. "You saved our lives."

"No. God had already washed you up on the beach. All I did was take care of visitors the way Gates told me to."

"Oh." Patrick cleared his throat. "Well, I'm sorry again about Jefferson. . . ."

Luke didn't answer.

"Where he's from, most people with dark skin were slaves until just a few years ago. You probably knew that, though."

Luke paused for a moment to look at the lantern. "I know what a slave is."

Suddenly Patrick noticed a wagon jerking across a hill behind them, approaching slowly in their direction. The wagon was piled high with wooden crates, and a man with a wild silver beard perched high in the driver's seat urged on a couple of tired-looking brown horses.

"Bet!" Luke called down toward the cottages. "Gates is here!"

Without another word Luke disappeared like a tornado down the stairway. Patrick followed as fast as he could, but Luke gripped the iron railing in both hands and flew down, taking the steps three or four at a time.

By the time Patrick caught up back at the cottages, the wild-haired man he had seen from the top of the lighthouse was just stepping down from the wagon. Luke grinned shyly at Gates, who returned a wink.

"Any trouble, Luke?" he asked. Patrick guessed Gates was old enough to be his grandfather; he looked weathered and tough.

"No trouble," reported Luke, patting one of the horses. "I ran into a couple of visitors, but I took care of them the way you told me."

The way Luke described them, Patrick felt like a piece of driftwood that had washed up on the beach, but he was glad to see Gates and the wagon. *A way back to the mainland, back to my family!*

Gates laughed. "Good for you, boy. We have to be hospitable." He picked up a couple of crates and handed one to each of the boys.

"I'm Henry Gates," he said, extending a crate for Patrick to carry instead of a hand to shake. "Make yourself useful."

Patrick took the case and nearly dropped from the weight. "I'm Patrick." He took a deep breath as he struggled forward with the crate. "The cabin boy from the ship I was on fell off during a storm and . . ."

Henry Gates turned back to pick up another crate, showing no sign of listening to Patrick's story.

"Well, that is, I . . ." Patrick faltered, and the wild-looking man turned back with a grin that revealed how many of his teeth were missing.

"Tell me your story over dinner, boy. You can carry one more, can't you?"

Without waiting for an answer, Gates piled another crate on top of the one Patrick already had.

"What's in these boxes?" Patrick grunted as he tried to follow Luke, but he couldn't quite see over the top of the crates.

"Just supplies," replied Luke, leading the way to one of the cottages. "Flour. Sugar. That sort of thing."

Jefferson came running from the direction of the beach.

"I heard the horses," he shouted, looking flushed.

"We need some help with these crates," Luke told him, nodding toward the wagon.

That night Bet served up her stew and boiled tea for them over her fire. Luke helped by adding what looked like odd, finger-sized sausages to her skillet. Bet still didn't speak but nodded and gestured in a private sign language to her nephew.

"It smells wonderful, Mrs. Bet," Patrick told her. Overhead, the beam of the lighthouse cast a strange glow every few seconds.

Bet raised her head at the mention of her name and smiled a shy grin. The woman could have been thirty or sixty; Patrick wasn't sure which. She seemed to be young and old all at once.

Gates took another large bite and whispered something in a strange language to Bet. She looked at the boys and laughed.

"What did he say?" Patrick wondered aloud.

Luke smiled. "He said you are enjoying the meal, but you probably have no idea what it is."

"Kangaroo meat," answered Patrick. "We've had that before."

"And the tea comes from the local tea tree bush," added Luke.

"But what's in these sausages?" asked Jefferson. "They're very good. They taste like almonds."

"You can call them sausages if you want." Luke laughed. "But they're witchetty grubs."

Jefferson stopped chewing. "Witchetty . . ."

"Grubs." Luke's grin was still spreading. "Big worms."

Jefferson choked and put a hand to his mouth, and Luke laughed until he cried.

Patrick's stomach turned a somersault, too, but he had already finished his grubs. *I hope they stay where they are*, he thought worriedly.

"You said you liked them, didn't you?" asked Luke.

"They're delicious," answered Jefferson. He looked at Bet, smiled, and covered his plate. "Never tasted better."

Gates chuckled and popped a witchetty grub into his mouth while he peppered Jefferson with questions. Who were the captain and the first mate of the *Star of Africa*? What was the cargo? When did they leave Dublin? Which ports had they called upon? How had they both fallen off the ship?

A cool breeze from the direction of the ocean made Patrick

shiver, and when he leaned closer to the fire, his grandmother's ring slipped out from behind his shirt on its string.

Gates stopped in midsentence and stared at Patrick. Or rather, at Patrick's ring.

"Well, now, that's an interesting piece. Where did you come upon it?"

Patrick hurried to slip it back inside his shirt. "It belonged to my grandmother."

"May I see it?" Gates held out his huge, gnarled hand.

Patrick hesitated, but he didn't want to appear rude. Slowly, he pulled the string necklace over his head and held out the ring.

"Reminds me of my wife's ring," clucked the old man as he turned it over in his hand. "Almost the same."

The light from the cooking fire glittered off the polished green stone in the center of the ring. Gates squeezed it in his hand as if trying to make it disappear. He gave the ring one last look before returning it to Patrick.

"My mother always said the ring wasn't valuable, but she treasured it because it belonged to my grandmother." Patrick took the ring back and replaced it around his neck. "She died before I was born."

"A plain ring, 'tis true. But I suspect there's more to it than you see."

Patrick gazed off across the darkening water and thought about his grandfather, the one he had never met. "My grandfather came to Australia, too," he told no one in particular. "Last we heard, he was living in a town on the Murray River."

"That so?" asked Gates. "And what would his name be?"

"I'm named for him. Patrick. Patrick McWaid."

The polite smile on Henry Gates's face froze, and he turned back to his food. "This is a good stew, Bet," he mumbled, stuffing another piece of meat into his mouth.

Bet said nothing, only pulled the charred teapot off the fire and poured another steaming cup.

Did I say something wrong? Patrick wondered. He looked at Luke when Gates started stirring furiously at the fire, but Luke only shrugged. Jefferson didn't seem to notice what had been going on, he was so busy eating.

"Would you be able to take us back to the mainland soon, sir?" Jefferson changed the subject. Everyone looked at him except Gates. "I was thinking maybe we could catch up with my ship. We don't have any money, but I'm sure . . ."

There was a long moment of silence as Gates continued to poke at the fire. Patrick felt for his grandmother's ring. *Don't get any ideas, Jefferson. I'm not trading.*

But Gates didn't look as if he had heard anything Jefferson said.

"Patrick McWaid," he whispered, then suddenly looked up. "So you're his grandson, eh? I should have guessed from the look of you. Well, I still owe him. We'll leave as soon as the horses are rested."

With that he stood up and hurried away to his cottage, leaving the others to finish dinner—and to wonder.

"Wait!" Patrick called after the man. "Do you know my grandfather?"

Gates stopped at the door to his cottage, his back to them. "I knew him a long time ago, boy. Haven't seen him in years." He disappeared into his cottage and shut the door.

"Please, can't you tell me more?" Patrick asked the closed door, then gave up and returned to the fire.

"What was that all about?" asked Jefferson.

"I don't know." Patrick looked to Luke for an answer. "How does he know my grandfather?"

Luke shrugged and tossed a piece of stew meat to his dogs, who snapped at it hungrily. "I know as much as you do."

Jefferson scraped his plate clean, keeping a worried eye on the dogs. "Well, at least we know we're getting a ride back to the mainland. Good work, Patrick."

Patrick reached for his ring again and frowned. Who was this strange man who somehow knew his grandfather?

CHAPTER 17

CROSSING BACKSTAIRS PASSAGE

True to his word, Henry Gates was up with the sun, clearing his throat and making enough noise to wake everyone up.

Patrick carefully folded the blanket he had been sleeping on in the clearing next to the cottages. *Maybe he'll tell me more about my grandfather now*, he thought.

"I suppose your Irish mother trained you to make your bed, did she?" Gates laughed as he hurried out of his cottage and saw the neatly folded blanket on his step.

Patrick wasn't sure how to take the man's teasing, so he picked up his bedroll. "Yes, sir. Do you want this loaded on the wagon?"

Gates stopped to look down at Patrick and put his hands on the boy's shoulders. "Now, look here, kid. I don't want you getting your hopes up. It takes a week to cross the island to where we can take a boat to the mainland, and my horses are tired to start with. We'll do our best to get you back to your ma. But I can't guarantee anything."

Patrick took a step backward. "I know that, sir. I'll be glad just to get to Adelaide, where I can catch up to my family. But can't you tell me about my grand—"

Gates held up a hand. "It's none of your concern, really, but I told your grandfather once that I would repay him for what he did for me. We were both . . . uh, working for the government. I was sick, and he took care of me. Gave me his food and probably saved my life."

"You were a prisoner, too?"

Gates crossed his arms and shifted from foot to foot. "Well, yes. I don't know what happened to McWaid after he was freed. Just tell him if you find him that this is partial payment from Boomer Gates."

The name almost struck Patrick as funny, but of course he couldn't laugh. Boomer Gates took the bedroll out of Patrick's hands and hurried away. He stopped in midstride and turned to squint at Patrick.

"Boomer is short for boomerang. Leastwise, that's what he used to call me. And glory, but you're a younger image of your grandfather."

"What's all the shouting this time of morning?" Jefferson complained from his bedroll next to the fire pit. He had almost rolled into the fire, but he didn't seem to care.

"Come on, sleepyhead." Patrick walked over to where Jefferson lay. "Do you remember where we're going today?"

He bent over and, without warning, yanked the blanket away.

"Hey!" yelled Jefferson. "You can't do that!"

"That's one way to get you up." Patrick laughed and sprinted over to where Gates was bridling his horses.

Jefferson bellowed again, but he was too slow, and Henry Gates turned from tying a harness to see what all the noise was about.

"Hasn't been so much racket on this island since Luke was a young boy." He looked around. "Luke? You coming along this trip?"

"Yeh, I'm coming," Luke called back from the other side of the cottages.

A few minutes later they had loaded the food sacks Bet had packed them, canvas sacks full of flatbread and salted kangaroo meat, along with jugs full of water. The dogs whimpered as Gates shook the reins, and his two horses trotted away from the lighthouse.

"Sorry, boys, but you can't come along," Luke told them. "You take care of Bet."

The trip across the long, wide island was more of a parade than Patrick could have imagined, with settlers coming out to meet them on the road almost every day. And when they did, everyone stopped to swap endless stories.

"Didn't you just come back the other way, Henry?" asked an islander on the second day, an older woman prodding a couple of sheep with a stick. She stared at them with toothless curiosity.

"Sure enough," Gates replied as he did to all the others. "But do you know who this is? Patrick McWaid's grandson. I'm taking him back over to the mainland."

Whether they even knew who Patrick's grandfather was, Patrick wasn't always sure, but everyone stared at him and Jefferson as if they were museum pieces.

"Don't mind him," Luke whispered on the third day as they pulled past a stooped man standing by the side of the road. "That's one of the island's first English settlers. Came here fifty years ago, when there were only pirates and sealers."

"It wasn't so bad back then," Gates put in as they continued to bump down the island's rutted main road. "A good deal more quiet. Now there are people everywhere, and more of them the farther east we go." He spread his hand out toward the hills ahead of them.

Their goal was Kingscote, one of the larger settlements toward the eastern end of the island. But that would be three or four more days of travel, and every time they stopped for the night at a settler's farmhouse, Gates knew the owners and had to linger to visit.

"Is there anyone he doesn't know on this island?" Patrick asked as they settled down in a sweet-smelling bed of hay the fourth night. Everyone else was already asleep.

The sixth and last day on the road was much like the first—bumpy, dusty, and slow. True to form, more and more people came out to stare and find out why Henry Gates was coming back along the road so soon.

As they rattled down a hill toward the sea, Patrick sat quietly and wondered about his grandfather, about the stories Gates told, and about his missing father. *How am I ever going to find Ma and Becky and Michael?* He wished for some way, any way, to tell them he wasn't dead.

And what about Conrad Burke? He tried to imagine what the man was doing in Australia, and why the sailors back in Fremantle had mentioned his name. *He can't really be following us, can he? Why would he go to all the trouble?*

It was hard to make sense of it all, especially when he felt so tired. Bumpy road or no, he fell into a fitful sleep.

Patrick awoke to a huge splash of water in his face. For an instant he imagined himself back in the ocean, swallowing a wave and sinking. A shark had grabbed his arm and was pulling.

"Come on, Irishman, wake up." Jefferson pulled him out of his bedroll and rolled him out on the sand while Patrick groaned and tried to figure out where he was. The sharks had been a dream; Jefferson was not.

"You fell asleep in the wagon last night," Jefferson told him. "I thought you might like a hand waking up."

Jefferson ran away with his empty bucket, leaving Patrick to roll over on the grass. He could hear the ocean again, but it was still nearly dark, with only a hint of pink in the sky over the water. Then he remembered what Gates had told them the night before. They would be sleeping on the beach near the boat Gates had arranged for. The mainland would be straight across the channel, only a short sail across the . . . what had he called it?

Backstairs Passage, he remembered, looking out at the waters of a sheltered bay. Out on the rocky beach, someone had pulled up a ship's lifeboat, the kind made for rowing or sailing. Gates was crouched under the mast, mumbling and working at some ropes.

Patrick took a deep breath as a patchwork sail went up and began to flap in the gentle morning breeze. He got up on his knees and waited for the old fear of the water to grip his stomach again.

"No more," he prayed quietly. "God, please take it away."

Patrick heard footsteps crunching on the rocky beach and turned to see Luke hobbling toward him, carrying a wicker basket with both hands. Jefferson followed with a box of supplies from the wagon.

"Are you finally awake?" asked Luke with a smile. "Thought we were going to have to load you on the boat in a basket."

"I'm awake, thanks to Jefferson." Patrick scrambled to his feet, checked to make sure the ring was still around his neck, and followed them down to the boat with his blankets in his arms.

"Let's shove off, gentlemen," bellowed Gates from his position at the steering tiller. "You two, get on board and stay out of the way. Luke, push us off into deeper water. Need any help?"

"No, I've got it." Luke paused for a moment to look back at the island while Patrick chose a seat on one of the four wide benches in the middle of the large, open peapod-shaped boat. There was plenty of room left to seat a dozen more people.

"Well, here we go again," said Jefferson, stepping toward the boat. A second later he was sprawling, one foot hooked over the edge of the boat and the other dangling in the water.

"Whoa!" he cried, grabbing for support. "Slippery rock."

Before Patrick could even move to help, Luke jumped out into the waist-deep water and boosted Jefferson up and into the boat to safety.

Soaked to the shoulders, Luke quietly returned to pushing off the boat as Jefferson found a place to sit and held on.

"Thanks, Luke." Jefferson looked back at him as if seeing the aborigine boy for the first time.

Luke grinned and nodded as he put his shoulder to the back of the boat. Once he had pushed them out far enough and jumped aboard himself, Gates pulled the sail in tightly.

"Here we go!" he announced. Gentle waves challenged them as they cut out of the small cove, past a set of guardian rocks, and beyond the friendly grip of the land. As the wind took the sail in its teeth and they heeled over, Patrick made himself reach out to touch the gurgling blue-green water.

"How far to the mainland?" he asked as the sail crackled above their heads.

Luke splashed the salty water into his own face. "Seven hours, maybe. If we get a good southwester, you'll be eating dinner in Victor Harbor."

Luke pointed to the tall ridge of cliffs looming ahead of them. As the sun rose higher over the land, it looked closer than Patrick had ever seen it before.

He studied the shore. *Dinner with Ma and Becky and Michael.*

"Now, Adelaide," said Jefferson a few hours later. "That's a real city." He sat back comfortably against the picnic basket in the afternoon sun. "Parks everywhere. Grand streets. Tall buildings."

Patrick listened to Luke and Jefferson talking about Australian cities as he scanned the cliffs for signs of anything that could be Victor Harbor. A small coastal sailing ship had already passed them at a distance. Gates had told them they would follow her in.

"Adelaide, eh? You've been there before?" asked Luke, trailing his hand in the water.

"Well . . . ah," Jefferson stuttered, "not exactly in person. You?"

"I've read about it."

Luke looked over at Gates as if for help, but the man was apparently snoozing under his wide-brimmed hat. Even half asleep, he kept their boat on course, following the schooner across Backstairs Passage. The wind was freshening but still as steady and fair as when they had left the island that morning.

"He's never been to Adelaide," Gates finally drawled. "When you get there, take a look around and see how many people look like Luke or Bet."

"What do you mean?" asked Patrick.

The man's eyes snapped open. "I mean Luke's people are dying out, plain and simple." He spit into the ocean. "And those who are still alive are living in camps on the outskirts of the towns. When I found Luke and Bet, they were like castoffs in their own land. Filthy shame, the way some people treat 'em."

A wave scooted under the back end of their boat, sending Jefferson off balance. Luke put out a hand to catch the older boy, and for a moment Jefferson looked down at the black hand on his arm.

"I'm sorry," whispered Jefferson, hardly loud enough to hear over the waves. "I didn't know."

Luke smiled slightly. "Don't worry about me. All I remember is growing up on the island."

"Well, boys." Gates shielded his eyes as the sun settled lower and off to their left. "Luke promised dinner in Victor Harbor. Looks as if he was right."

"Won't my mates on the *Star of Africa* be surprised to see me?" Jefferson rubbed his hands together.

"If the ship is still there, you mean," replied Patrick. "Maybe they've moved on."

"We'll find out soon enough," Gates continued. "Storm being the way it was, they probably ended up in the nearest shelter. That'd be Victor Harbor, right behind Granite Island."

"They'll still be there." Jefferson looked more sure of himself the closer they got to the low shore and the town's collection of buildings. "Just wait and see."

They didn't have to wait long. Only minutes later Patrick pointed excitedly toward a cluster of four or five larger ships, all anchored in the harbor behind the protection of a small, barren island.

"There it is!" said Patrick. "The only one painted white."

"I knew it." Jefferson sat up straight and beamed. "I *knew* it would be here."

As they sailed closer, though, Patrick's face fell. Even he could tell something was very wrong with the *Star of Africa*.

CHAPTER 18

DISCOVERY IN VICTOR HARBOR

"The ship looks horrible," Patrick said finally.

Jefferson nodded seriously as he took in the damage, too. "Like it got caught in a giant spider's web. All those broken lines . . ."

"And one of the masts is missing."

"They're lucky they didn't end up wrecked," put in Gates, "the way the *Fides* did back in 1860."

They slipped into the fleet of crippled ships. Men were working on two of them. Others, like the *Star*, seemed almost deserted, leaning over to one side or another, or barely afloat.

"Things can't be all bad." Patrick stood as they pulled up beside the *Star of Africa*. "I see Ebony on deck. I'll bet that means my brother is going to be right there with him."

Luke looked up with concern at the furry brown shape above them as he helped tie up their boat. A few minutes later, they all stood together in the familiar salon of the *Star of Africa*, surrounded by a welcoming group of sailors. A few clapped Jefferson on the back and began asking him questions, but Patrick had only one thing on his mind.

"My ma." Patrick faced the ship's first mate, a plain, older man with touches of gray in his hair and a kindly face. "What do you know?"

The man looked down at the floor and shook his head.

"I'm afraid they've left, lad. She and your sister and brother."

"What do you mean, left?"

"We all thought you were dead, given the circumstances. The skipper even conducted a funeral service for you two. And a first-rate one it was, too, with—"

"Where did they go?" Patrick interrupted him. "When did they leave?"

The mate turned to another sailor. "Tommy, do you remember when the boy's family left the ship? Mrs. McWaid and the two children?"

"Yesterday or the day before." One of the sailors stopped listening to Jefferson's stories long enough to guess. "No, it was yesterday morning. Said something about a grandfather."

"So they're going to Ech—" Patrick turned to Luke for help.

"Echuca," finished Luke.

"I have to go after them, Jefferson." Patrick pushed through the crowd gathered around the other boy, who was still telling his story about the storm and the sharks with grand gestures and sound effects. "I have to go find them. Jefferson?" Patrick caught him by the shoulder. "Did you hear what he said about Ma? I have to go find her right away."

"Pardon my saying so, Master Patrick," put in the first mate, "but you're going to need some new clothes if you don't want people to think you're a castaway. I'd recommend dinner, as well."

Patrick looked down at his ripped shirt, the ragged open knee of his pants, and his worn boots. The sailor was right. And despite his best efforts to keep it quiet, his growling stomach sounded like Ebony the sun bear.

"Dinner sounds good," said Henry Gates, who had been standing behind Patrick the whole time, listening. "It sounds very good."

At least dinner gave Jefferson more of a chance to tell his story. Even Luke joined in when Jeff reached the part about being lost in the cave.

Patrick, though, was silent. *They still think I'm dead*, he told himself, picking at the lamb stew with carrots. It was the best meal he had tasted in weeks, but he looked uneasily toward the door. *And*

I'm just sitting here, having dinner.

"You have to eat," Gates told him as if reading his mind.

Patrick reluctantly took another bite. "I have to leave as soon as I can, sir. I need to find them."

Gates shook his head. "You don't even know for certain where your mother is. I think it would be best for you to stay on the ship."

"No, sir. I've made up my mind. I'm going to Echuca, same as they are. That's where I'll find them, with my grandfather—if he's there."

Gates started to say something, then changed his mind and sighed. "You not only look like the old codger, you sound very much like him." He rose to his feet, then reached into his pocket, pulled out a silver coin, and pressed it into Patrick's hand. "Here."

"But—" Patrick started to protest, but Gates wagged his finger to stop him.

"Did you for a moment consider how you were going to get there?" asked Gates. "You don't just jump on a riverboat without paying, young man."

"I . . . I . . ." Patrick stuttered. "You can't . . ." He tried again.

"Of course I can, but don't you go wasting that money." He pointed at Patrick in a friendly warning. "First thing in the morning, you catch the tramway to Goolwa, and from there you get on a Murray River paddle-wheeler to Echuca. With the rains we've had, I hear there are already boats traveling the river."

Patrick nodded. The coin Gates had given him, a florin, would be more than enough for the ticket.

"And when you finally catch up to your grandfather," Gates continued, "you be sure to tell him from me that now he and Boomer Gates are even. Got that?"

"Thank you," Patrick whispered, but Gates had already turned for the door.

"Luke!" Gates called, and Luke looked up from petting Ebony. "Time for us to take our leave. Thanks for the meal, gentlemen."

Patrick looked over at the boy who had become his friend so quickly. "Can't you wait for morning to leave?" he asked.

Luke grinned but shook his head. "We'll sleep on the boat."

Even Jefferson put out his hand. "Ah . . . thanks for all you did." He looked nervous. "I'm much obliged to you for all your help."

"Glad to do it, mate." Luke pumped Jefferson's hand, winked at Patrick, and turned to go. "Oh, and Patrick—"

"Yes?"

"I'm sure you'll find your pa soon."

Soon. Patrick watched Luke and Gates climb back into their boat, and he found himself wishing they would stay just a little longer. He watched as the sail turned into a speck on the horizon.

When exactly is "soon"?

Patrick awoke early the next morning with the same question on his mind.

At least I'm going in the right direction, he told himself. With a clean set of clothes from the sailors and Henry Gates's coin in his pocket, he cleared his throat to say good-bye to Jefferson.

"Gates was right," Jefferson told him as he rowed closer to the jetty that pointed into the deeper water of Victor Harbor. "I don't think it's a good idea for you to be going on alone, either."

"We talked about that last night." Patrick got ready to stand up.

"True, but"—Jefferson fended their rowboat away from the wharf pilings—"I'm actually going to miss you. I feel badly that I'm not going with you from here."

Did he say what I think he did?

Patrick waited until a larger wave picked up their small boat, then jumped out onto a ladder on the dock when it was highest.

"I'll be all right." Patrick stood on the wharf and looked down at his friend, bouncing up and down in the rowboat. "But I couldn't have made it without you, Jeff."

Jefferson grinned and waved before he rowed slowly away.

Patrick knew he would miss the older boy. *Even if he's trouble sometimes*, he thought.

He pulled his traveling bag over his shoulder, a small canvas seabag Jefferson had given him filled with clothes and other things the sailors said they didn't need.

"Bye" came Jefferson's voice from down below, and Patrick walked faster, away from the water.

I don't want to miss the train, he told himself, even though he had no idea when the train would leave.

Beyond the landing was a rough downtown, a cluster of unpainted wooden shacks and two warehouses where trains were loaded with freight for the river port of Goolwa. Patrick had no problem picking out the station, if one could call it that. It was not much more than a modest shed next to the tracks, with a hand-painted sign above the door.

Patrick pushed open the door, then shuffled up to a woman sitting at a table inside the one-room building.

"Could you please—" He tried to make his voice sound lower than usual. "Please, could you tell me when the next train leaves for Goolwa?"

"Twenty minutes," she answered, not even looking up. "And the tramway stops in Port Elliot and Middleton."

"Thank you. I'd like one ticket, please."

"Shilling and sixpence." As the ticket woman took his money, she looked up for the first time, and her look turned suspicious. "And where would your parents be?"

Patrick knew he would have to explain himself.

"My family's in Echuca," he told her as sweetly as he could manage. "A friend of our family, Henry Gates, arranged for me to join them."

"Gates?" The woman seemed surprised at the mention of the name. "That good-for-nothing's a friend of yours?"

Patrick retreated out of the station house as quickly as he could, ticket in hand. He sat quietly next to the station barn, trying to stay out of the way of the busy men who came with carts full of crates from the harbor. They shouted and jockeyed their wagons around, then thick-armed young men wrestled and dragged the cargo into place, ready for loading.

Patrick searched the flat land along the coast for the plume of steam and black smoke that would show where the train was. Finally he saw something coming down the track in their direction, but no smoke.

What can that be?

Five minutes later it was obvious there wasn't going to be a steam train to Goolwa. Instead, Patrick saw a team of two powerful horses coming down the tracks in their direction, pulling a single large carriage. Seven or eight people rode under the shelter of a sun canopy, open on both sides.

"This is the train for Goolwa?" Patrick asked a woman with a yellow parasol who was sitting near him.

"We call it the tramway." The woman looked behind him, as if she expected to see his parents. Patrick didn't try to explain but waited patiently for the horses to be turned around and hitched up again to take the train back in the other direction. After he showed his ticket, he climbed aboard with a couple of other passengers and found a seat on one of the four rows of hard wooden benches.

"It may not be the fastest way to get around," explained the man who was taking their tickets, "but we'll make Goolwa in two and a half hours."

As he took Patrick's ticket, the man gave Patrick the same look he had been getting ever since they arrived in Victor Harbor. "Say, you're not traveling alone, are you, boy?"

Patrick was about to answer when he heard a shout from out on the track, then the flash of someone running up beside the tramway and hopping on.

"Almost left without me!" said the late arrival, catching his breath.

Patrick looked up in surprise. "Jeff! What are you doing here?"

"You can't get rid of me that easily." Jefferson flashed one of his wide grins and showed his ticket to the conductor. "And since I was supposed to be dead, I talked the captain into letting me go with you. He even loaned me money for a ticket."

"Grand!"

"I had to promise I'd be back in three weeks, before by the end of May at the latest. Captain figures they'll be ready to sail again by then. That gives us plenty of time to find your ma."

"It should be no trouble, Jeff. We'll be there in a few days."

"In Echuca."

"Yes. Echuca." Patrick liked the way the name rolled off his tongue. "Echuca," he repeated softly, just as a set of iron fingers clamped painfully over his shoulders.

"Young McWaid," said a voice that turned Patrick's blood cold. "What an astonishing surprise."

CHAPTER 19

ESCAPE TO MURRAY RIVER

Patrick knew who had just slipped into the carriage behind Jefferson, but he was afraid to look. It couldn't be! Here, halfway around the world . . .

Conrad Burke!

"I was hoping to catch up with you on the west coast in Fremantle when you first arrived," said Burke, "but apparently you left suddenly. I followed in the next available ship."

Patrick said nothing, only stared in disbelief at the man with the piercing black eyes who was suddenly sitting next to him. He wished he could look away and make him disappear.

"Then I heard you were washed overboard and lost at sea, just as your father was."

"They told us he died of consumption." Patrick finally found his voice.

Burke looked surprised, but only for a moment. "Ah yes, but we know better, now, do we not?"

We do? Patrick wondered what the man knew, but he kept silent. *What about the sailors who mentioned Burke back in Fremantle? Was he out looking for Pa while we were there?*

Their driver urged the horses to a slow, steady pace, and they began rolling down the tracks.

"In any case, here you are, and sure you're looking fit and well.

You must tell me your amazing story!"

Telling his story to Burke was the last thing Patrick wanted to do. He could scream or yell for help, but what would he say?

"I'm Jefferson Pitney." Jeff smiled and put out his hand. "You must be from Ireland, too."

"Perceptive! Forgive me for not introducing myself. Conrad Burke. Delighted. Yes, I'm from Dublin, in the employ of the *Evening Telegraph*. Friend of the family. I've had myself assigned here to the Australian colony to produce a series of articles on effects of the gold rush."

Patrick frowned. *And I'm the King of England.*

"Really?" Jefferson looked interested. "Sounds like an exciting job."

Burke nodded and continued his story. He could be charming when he wanted to be. "Quite. And now by remarkable felicity, Patrick and I find that our paths have crossed once more, after coming all this way."

Patrick wished he could tell Jefferson who the man really was, that Burke was looking for Pa, but Conrad Burke's bold smile seemed to tie Patrick's tongue in place.

"Tell me, young man, what are the chances of meeting a friend like this, and so far from home, at that?"

Jeff shook his head in amazement. "I sure don't know, Mr. Burke. Million to one chance, I suppose."

"Perhaps more, lad. Tell me about your ship."

Patrick looked for a way of escape while Jefferson chatted happily about the storm, being lost at sea, Kangaroo Island, and Henry Gates. Burke seemed most interested to hear the part about how the boys were hoping to catch up with Mrs. McWaid.

"Is that a fact!" sang Mr. Burke. "Perhaps I could even write a story on this amazing adventure for the *Evening Telegraph*! What do you think, Patrick?"

"It's your article, Mr. Burke." Patrick was feeling more and more sick to his stomach. *This isn't right!* he thought. But he couldn't think of a way to explain it to Jeff, not in front of Burke, so he just stared glumly out at the glittering ocean as they followed the coastline.

"You think they're in Echuca, then?" Burke sounded more than interested in hearing about Patrick's grandfather, and Jefferson was only too glad to fill him in.

"Ow!" said Jefferson, partway through his story. "You kicked me, Patrick."

"Sorry." Patrick tried to signal with his eyes, but Jefferson only gave him a puzzled look and kept chatting.

"We're pretty sure it's Echuca, aren't we, Patrick?"

"Uh . . ." Patrick wondered how he could stall the conversation, or better yet, jump off the train and run away. "It could be, but you never know. I'm really not sure."

Jefferson squinted and wrinkled his forehead. "But I thought—"

"You know how it is," continued Patrick quickly. "They could be in Sydney by now, or maybe Adelaide. They could be in one of a thousand places. . . ."

At last the slow-moving tram pulled into a weathered town and came to a stop next to a building that might have been a flour mill. A man on the covered platform got up from his seat on a sack of flour, dusted himself off, and climbed aboard.

"Goolwa?" Burke stood up and looked around expectantly. "Not much to the place, is there?"

"Port Elliot," announced their driver. "Then Middleton, then Goolwa."

"Of course," replied Burke.

Patrick looked around again for a way of escape, but Burke seemed to keep a viselike grip on Jefferson as they continued on. *And what would I do anyway?* Patrick wondered. *Where would we hide?* He tried to map out a plan in his head as they passed through Middleton, which was something like Port Elliot, and then neared the end of the line.

Goolwa seemed even busier than Victor Harbor, with a bustling main street and a lively collection of stone buildings, warehouses, and wooden shacks. Two half-finished riverboats were being built near the riverbank, and at least four small riverboats were tied up at the wharf. A couple were belching black smoke from their smokestacks.

"Coming up to Goolwa," announced their driver. "If you don't plan to catch a Murray River paddle steamer today, you can overnight at either the Australasian or the Corlo Hotel. Our last stop is here at the post office. Stay out of the sun under the veranda, if you like."

Their driver pointed to a building on their left with a wide, shady front porch. As they jerked to a stop, Patrick knew he had only a second to make his plan work. While the small crowd of passengers and Burke turned to step out of the tram to the left, he grabbed Jefferson's arm and yanked him down to the ground on the right, on the other side of the tracks.

"Wha—?" began Jefferson, but Patrick clamped his hand over the other boy's mouth and ducked his head. They rolled underneath, and Patrick dragged Jefferson out behind the tram.

"What are you doing?" whispered Jefferson as soon as they were clear. "Are you crazy?"

Patrick didn't have time to answer; he just pulled Jefferson by the arm behind him as they scrambled around to the other side of the stables where the tramway horses were kept. Patrick never stopped praying that Burke wouldn't see them.

"See him?" Patrick leaned against the back of the stable to catch his breath.

"You mean your friend from Ireland? I don't—"

"Listen, I don't have time to explain everything," Patrick interrupted, "but Burke's not a friend. He's definitely not a friend. He's after my Pa."

"What are you talking about? I thought he worked for a newspaper."

"Jeff, you just have to trust me. Burke is not a nice man. He's the one who put my father in jail."

"Him?" Jefferson peeked around the building.

"I can't prove it yet, but I think he tried to have my father killed and something went wrong. That's why Pa escaped."

"And he hates your pa so much that he followed him all the way to Australia?"

"I can't explain that. But I'm sure he's using us to try to find Pa again."

Jefferson didn't look convinced. "If that's what he's doing, he's going to an awful lot of trouble. . . ."

They both looked around the corner of the stable again, and Patrick realized they would have to run out into the open, down a short stretch of railroad tracks, to reach the wharf. At least it was only a short sprint from the stables to the waiting paddle steamers, where a steep bank on the right dropped down to the river. Maybe they could hide there, beyond the tracks that led out to the end of the wharf.

"Your friend's looking for us," Jefferson softly warned.

Burke was standing in the middle of the station platform, holding a carpetbag and shielding his eyes from the bright sun. He pivoted on his heel and for a moment looked their way. He did not look pleased. They both pulled their heads back.

"Why are we hiding?" asked Jefferson. "He knows where we're going, and we know where he's going."

"Yes, thanks to—" Patrick bit his tongue. "Well, anyway, maybe we'll get on different boats, and then we can warn my mother."

They heard footsteps behind them and whirled around to see a young boy coming their way, pushing a rolling barrel hoop with a stick.

"Hey, kid—" Jefferson reached out and grabbed the hoop to stop it, and the boy skidded to a stop.

"That's mine!" protested the boy, who couldn't have been older than Michael.

Jefferson held on to the hoop and looked around. "We just want to know about the riverboats. Which one goes to Echuca?"

The boy tried to grab his hoop back, then crossed his arms and glared at Jefferson.

"Jeff," protested Patrick, "don't tease him that way."

Jefferson kept holding the hoop behind his back, waiting for an answer.

"How do I know?" the boy finally said. "Some of them go up the Murray River, some of them turn off on the Darling or the Murrumbidgee. Why don't you ask them yourselves?"

Jefferson frowned and looked over at the four paddle steamers before he handed back the hoop.

"You could have just asked him," Patrick pointed out.

Jefferson shrugged and checked the street again as the little boy ran away. "Uh-oh. Here comes Burke, and it looks as though he's going to grab the boy with the hoop."

Patrick was about to scoot around to the other side of the stable, but Jefferson held his arm.

"Here, lad!" they heard Burke shout. "Would you like to earn a penny?"

Patrick sighed quietly and got ready to run again. If they had to, they could outrun Burke, but for how long?

"He's leaving," reported Jefferson.

A moment later they were sprinting over the short stretch of railroad tracks that led down the wharf. Patrick looked only once over his shoulder. He couldn't see Burke anywhere, but he tripped over a railroad tie and tumbled down a steep dirt slope to the riverbank below.

"Patrick!" cried Jefferson, but Patrick couldn't stop rolling. He ended up in a heap on the bank below, dazed and dizzy but unhurt. A small, gnomelike man who had been sleeping in a chair on the side deck of the first paddle steamer jerked awake.

"Eh?" he cleared his throat and set the chair back down on its four feet. "What are you boys doing?"

"Please, sir." Patrick got to his feet and glanced back up at the wharf, waiting for Burke to follow. A few people looked down curiously, then went on their way. "We need to go to Echuca."

"You waiting for someone?" The man looked at them suspiciously and tugged at his double chin.

Patrick shook his head. "No, we're not."

"Well, you can't—" But the man stopped and grinned when he noticed the large coin Patrick held out, part of the change from the money Henry Gates had given him. "On second thought, maybe you can. But where are your parents?"

Patrick was prepared this time. "We're hoping to meet them in Echuca."

"Then welcome to the *Lady Elisabeth*." He took the coin and waved his hand as if to open an imaginary door, and they both climbed on board. "My name's Prentice. Our boilers are firing up, and we'll be off within the hour."

Letting out his breath, Patrick nodded and took up a station on the river side of the main deck, just around the corner from the main two-story deckhouse. Their boat was much like the other three tied up on the other side of the wharf, each with a set of covered paddle wheels on the side and a wheelhouse up front and on top, where the captain steered. To their right, the muddy brown Murray River flowed slowly past, looking very much like hot chocolate.

"They're not nearly as big as the Mississippi riverboats back home." Jefferson sniffed the sweet-smelling breeze. "Like the ones in Memphis, down on Peale Street Landing. Why, those were so big, you could set three or four of these boats right on top of one and still have room."

"Well, this isn't the Mississippi River."

"Let's take a look around," suggested Jefferson, but Patrick held him back.

"Not until we're sure Burke doesn't follow us."

A family with small children boarded next. They were followed by a couple of men carrying boxes of tools, then a man dragging two very loud sheep. After that they watched as men loaded a piano aboard with a lot of grunting and complaining.

"Crazy thing to be bringing up the river, if you ask me," said one.

"Long as you get paid at the end of the day," replied another, "what's it to you?"

After the piano came men with barrels of flour, kegs of beer, even a sewing machine, which the red-faced complainer and his partner brought aboard last.

"Maybe he's getting on one of the other boats," whispered

Patrick, still hiding around the corner.

"So why are we whispering?" asked Jefferson, taking a look. He pulled back quickly and poked Patrick in the ribs with his elbow.

"What?"

"Your friend is coming this way."

Patrick looked out to see Burke slipping down the bank, obviously on his way to their boat.

They glanced around, and Patrick pointed at a ladder.

"Up there."

They climbed the ladder but kept low when they reached the top, all the time watching for Burke. Down on the deck, they could see the man stepping aboard, then gesturing at the deckhand, as if showing him how tall the two boys were.

"He's going to tell Burke we're here," Patrick worried.

But the deckhand only paused, looked over his shoulder, and shook his head. Just the same, Burke shoved past him and onto the deck. Jefferson and Patrick scooted around the narrow top deck around the wheelhouse like crabs as Burke searched below. A moment later Burke came flying up the same ladder they had and burst into the captain's wheelhouse. Patrick and Jefferson ducked as low as they could on the opposite side of the wheelhouse, just out of sight.

"Captain, I'm looking for a pair of runaways," boomed Burke. "Someone said they're on your boat."

"You talked to Prentice below?" answered a gruff, hoarse voice. Patrick was afraid to look as they crouched on the deck. If either of the men had cared to, they could have looked over the edge to see Patrick and Jefferson hiding.

"He wouldn't tell me anything," Burke replied. "But as I said—"

"You have a ticket, mister?" interrupted the old man.

"Of course not, but . . ."

"If Prentice couldn't tell you anything and you have no ticket, then there's nothing else I can do for you." The door opened again. "Now it's half eleven, and we must be off. Of course, you knew that?"

Burke sputtered, and Patrick heard the man retreating down the ladder to the deck below.

"Where did he go?" Patrick whispered to Jeff, who was hanging over the edge to catch a peek.

"He's talking to the deckhand again."

Patrick groaned.

Just then the captain pulled on his steam whistle. Patrick jumped.

"We're off, Prentice!" the captain shouted out his window, down at the deck. For a brief second he glanced at the two boys—but turned immediately back to his steering wheel.

He saw us! thought Patrick as they pushed away from Goolwa's wharf and caught the current. The twin paddle wheels began to churn the river into chocolate foam, and they turned away and back upstream. Twenty feet from the wharf they caught sight of Burke, staring at them from the muddy riverbank.

Jefferson waved innocently. "See you later, Mr. Burke!"

Patrick tried to grab Jefferson's hand, but he looked at the river as it widened between them and Burke, and he waved, too.

"We sure fooled him, didn't we?" Jefferson seemed to enjoy the game, but Patrick wasn't so sure. Burke ran to one of the other boats.

"For now."

Prentice the deckhand stood below them at the foot of the ladder. "There's no riding up there!" he warned them, and Patrick quickly slipped down to the deck below. Prentice caught him by the shoulders.

"I don't know who you boys are, but that fella looked like a lawman to me. The Old Man, he doesn't always like lawmen." Prentice squinted through kind eyes, edged by wrinkles from the sun.

"Thanks," answered Patrick. "We really are on the way to see my ma in Echuca. And that man wasn't a policeman."

"No need to explain," said Prentice.

"He's the Old Man?" Jefferson nodded toward the wheelhouse.

"Yeh," Prentice answered, "but don't go up there again. Besides the law, he doesn't take much to children."

Above them, the Old Man looked straight ahead, steering a course for the center of the wide lake of a river around Goolwa. With his enormous hands, he looked like a boxer, well-proportioned and powerful. His hair was bleached silver, his skin tanned and leathery. Patrick guessed he was probably even older than he looked.

"What's his real name?" Patrick wanted to know.

Prentice looked puzzled, as if that were an odd question, and scratched his chubby, grizzled chin. "Never actually heard it spoken. Everyone just calls him Old Man."

He left them to watch the wide, grand river, framed in the distance by a low-lying shore. As they continued upriver and began to carve a snakelike course through the land, the shore drew in and rose into rugged, rusty limestone cliffs. In time, the cliffs gave way to tangles of short, stunted eucalyptus trees. And just before dark, a black swan took off ahead of them with an angry squawk, leading them around another twisted bend of the river.

"This is the most beautiful place I've ever seen," whispered Jefferson as the Old Man lit a powerful pair of kerosene searchlights above them. "It kind of reminds me of home, back on the White River."

"You don't say?" Patrick was enjoying the show, too.

Jefferson nodded. "Scenery's different, but the water looks about the same. Next town we get to, I think I'm going to write a letter to the cousins I'm supposed to have in Sydney to ask them if I can come live with them."

"I thought you had to report back to your ship."

"I do, but after that."

"You never told me you had relatives in Australia."

"They're not really relatives. One of my sisters married a fellow, and they're *his* cousins—something of that sort. But they're here in Australia, somewhere. Didn't I tell you that before?"

Patrick shook his head and looked up to see the sparks drifting out of the two smokestacks. The *slap, slap, slap* of the twin paddle wheels was almost soothing. To their left the sun had just set in a fiery orange ball over the dunes, leaving behind only ripples of purple and gold on the water. Above, the Old Man paused to stare down his sharp wedge of a nose at them for a moment before he disappeared once more into his wheelhouse.

"What's that fire on the shore?" Jefferson asked Prentice as they paddled their way upstream through the gathering darkness. They could see two or three dark figures huddled around the fire, watching them silently.

"Aborigines," Prentice replied without looking. "Used to be lots more on this stretch of the river, years ago. Not so many now. They keep on the move."

Patrick wondered if Luke's family had come from this place. He looked up at the stars, and the Southern Cross, so clear now, seemed to wink at him like an old friend as another set of bright lights came up behind them. Prentice and the Old Man had noticed, as well.

"I'll bet that's the *Beachworth*," Prentice called upstairs, "trying to beat us into Echuca. They were getting steam up as we were leaving Goolwa."

"Beat us?" grumbled the Old Man. He pushed up his sleeve, exposing a purple tattoo of a kangaroo holding up two fists. "Go tell Kang Po in the engine room to stoke it up."

Prentice disappeared to shout at the man who tended the *Lady Elisabeth*'s boilers, and Patrick followed in curiosity. Kang Po was stripped to the waist, sweating as if he had just come out of a sauna. Prentice seemed to think that the louder he shouted at him, the more he would understand. But no matter what Prentice said, the reaction from the small, powerful-looking Chinese man was the same.

"Too much!" insisted Kang Po, puffing out his cheeks and imitating an explosion with his hands. "Too much and it blows!"

"I don't care if the valves are popping," Prentice yelled. "Old Man says to sprag 'em."

Prentice pressed his palms together and made a hissing sound, showing Kang Po that he wanted him to put something heavy on the safety valves so they could go faster.

Kang Po wiped the sweat from his forehead, shook his head, and turned back to his steam engine.

"Too much and it blows?" worried Patrick, returning to the deck.

Jefferson shrugged.

They could tell from the sound of the water underneath that they were picking up speed, but it was not enough to stay ahead of the other riverboat. After nearly an hour of cat-and-mouse tag in the darkness, the brightly lit *Beachworth* pulled up beside them.

"It's him again," said Jefferson quietly, but Patrick had already caught sight of Conrad Burke leaning casually against a small boat on the rear deck of his paddle-wheeler. He was staring straight at them, and Patrick shivered.

"Let's go inside to the salon," Patrick told Jefferson. He glanced overhead and saw the smoke roaring out of their smokestacks with a fiery glow. Still, they were only even with the *Beachworth*, and neither pulled ahead. A low-hanging branch caught the side of the *Lady Elisabeth* as they cut a corner of another bend in the river.

"It's not enough!" Patrick heard Prentice shouting down to the boiler room, and Kang Po yelled back something Patrick couldn't understand. A moment later Prentice rushed into the salon, pulling down lanterns from the wall and dumping the kerosene into a bucket.

"What are you doing?" asked Patrick. "What's going on?"

"Never you mind," replied the man, hurrying on toward the boiler room.

"He's stoking up the boiler," explained Jefferson. "Gets real hot when they dump in kerosene, bacon grease, anything liquid that burns. We'll go faster."

"Faster? But—" Patrick looked through the rough-cut plaid curtains at the other riverboat. Sure enough, they were inching slowly ahead of the *Beachworth* again. He listened to the yelling between Kang Po and Prentice for a few minutes and imagined what he would do if the big steam boiler blew up.

CHAPTER 20

SPECIAL DELIVERY

"I think maybe we lost the race." Patrick searched the river ahead of them first thing the next morning, but no other paddle steamers were in sight. Prentice hurried by.

"Don't tell that to the Old Man," said the deckhand. "He's in a powerful bad mood since the *Beachworth* passed us in the night."

Patrick let out his breath, glad he wouldn't have to worry about blowing up anymore.

By the third and fourth days, he and Jefferson were actually enjoying life on the river. They woke in the salon to the gentle *swish-swish* of the waterwheels, or sometimes a crazy screech from a bird somewhere above them. To pass the time they helped Kang Po stack wood in the boiler room, and then watched the cook, whose name was Albert, clean fish for breakfast. Mostly the main dish was delicious Murray River cod, which they picked up in the towns or from aborigines who stood in wooden bark canoes along the river edges. But all that time, they never saw the Old Man up close.

"Doesn't he like people?" Jefferson asked Prentice on the fifth afternoon.

The man sucked on his lips, thinking of his answer. "It's not that, exactly. He's just different. Knows every bend of this river— where it's deep enough to float, where the sandbars are. Even when there's no moon. He prefers to steer most of the time; I'm not sure when he sleeps."

"Or even *if* he sleeps," added the cook, scraping another portion of fish onto their plates.

Prentice just laughed and looked nervously in the direction of the wheelhouse. "I'm going to take him some lunch."

Jefferson ate his fish out on the side deck, staring into the tangles of eucalyptus trees that now crowded the riverbanks. Often other dark trees hung out over the water, as if peering at their reflections. And once in a while they would slip by other steamers going down the narrow river, and the men on the two ships would greet each other with a friendly salute or wave. Patrick was afraid to think of where Burke's ship might have gone, or even whether it was now ahead or behind them.

"Prentice said we'll be in Echuca pretty soon," Patrick told Jefferson, who nodded absently.

"We'll find your ma there," answered Jefferson. "I know we will."

Echuca was something like the other river towns, only larger and busier—much busier—even in the late afternoon.

"River's already rising for the winter," Prentice told them as he stepped up to the huge wooden wharf. "See, it's built tall to match the big up and down of the river. Dry in the summer, wet in the winter."

Patrick shook his head. "These backward seasons are hard to get used to. Here it is the beginning of May, and it's autumn."

Prentice laughed. "You'll get used to it, boy. Just be glad it's already rained. Last year we sat here for three months, twenty feet lower than we are now. This boat will float on a heavy dew, but we didn't even have that."

I'm not going to sit here, Patrick told himself, waiting for the boat to be tied up. *I have to find Ma.*

"Look at all that wool." Jefferson pointed to hundreds of square bales pressed tightly and marked with the names of odd-sounding places like Conargo, Booroorban, and Dahwilly. The wharf was alive with shouting men and horses, steam engines, and cranes swinging everywhere. There must have been at least six other paddle steamers loading and unloading, vessels of all different sizes and shapes. From somewhere up the river Patrick could hear the whine of a sawmill.

"See the *Beachworth*?" he asked Jefferson quietly.

Jefferson checked the lineup of paddle steamers again and nodded. "Right over there."

Patrick sighed at the thought of who had been aboard the other boat, but he knew there was nothing he could do about it now. "How many hotels did you say there are here?" he asked Prentice.

"Not a bad little town," Prentice answered. "Sixteen hotels, fifteen beer halls, five grocers, even a brand-new roller-skating hall."

"No kidding?" Jefferson looked interested. "I've heard of roller-skating. Been meaning to try it sometime."

"We don't have time for that, Jeff," Patrick reminded him. "We have to find my family before Burke does."

Jefferson nodded and got ready to jump to the wharf while Prentice swung a plank over. "I'm still not sure you need to worry about that fellow here in Australia, Patrick. All we have to do is find your mother."

"You still don't understand, Jeff." Patrick looked up at the fine brick warehouses and customs buildings that lined the waterfront. "Burke is a snake, and he's using us to find my pa."

"First place I'd check would be the Bridge Hotel," Prentice called after them.

Another steamer whistled long and low as it approached town, and Patrick stepped hurriedly over big iron hooks and coils of rope on the wharf. As Prentice had explained, finding the Bridge Hotel wasn't hard at all. Patrick tripped over a rut in the muddy street as they walked up to the grand-looking two-story building. He picked himself up quickly and ran in under the wide, covered veranda, through the front door, and up to the hotel clerk.

"We're looking for my mother," Patrick began, smiling politely across the hotel front desk at a round, pink-cheeked woman, "Mrs. McWaid. Is she—they told us she might be here."

The woman looked over the counter at Patrick and Jefferson, and she wrinkled her eyebrows in concern. "And who would you be?"

"Her son," answered Patrick.

The woman motioned for a man to join her, and they both stared.

Patrick fidgeted. *Maybe if I ask her again, she'll understand me*, he thought. *Maybe she's not used to Irish accents*.

"Mrs. McWaid?" he tried once more, this time more slowly. "Sarah McWaid?"

The woman, her face a human question mark, looked to her friend.

"What do you think?" she asked the man.

He shook his head and shrugged. "She never mentioned another child."

"I don't understand," said Patrick, standing on his tiptoes. "Is my mother not here?"

"She was," explained the woman. "She *was* here, but she checked out this afternoon."

Jefferson groaned and hit the side of his head with his hand. "Not again. We traveled all this way and missed your mother by just a few hours?"

"Actually," said the man, pulling a pocket watch out of his vest pocket, "they checked out just before noon." He eyed Patrick suspiciously.

"I really am her son," Patrick tried to make them understand. "But she just doesn't know that I . . . or rather, she thinks I fell overboard, and actually, I *did*, but . . ." His voice trailed off as he realized how ridiculous the story sounded.

The woman nodded her head. "Yes, I can see the resemblance now. Particularly to your mother. In any case, I believe your father was able to catch up with her."

Patrick's jaw dropped open. "Did you say my *father*?"

"That's correct," said the man. "He came running in here this forenoon, much the same way you did. Fortunately, I believe he caught up with them before they departed Echuca."

"My father!" Patrick bounced on his toes in excitement. "My brother, Michael, and Becky were with her then, too?"

"And the orphaned koala someone on the street gave them." This time the woman didn't look happy. "You should have seen what that beast did to the lobby curtains. Fortunately, your father paid for the damages."

"He did?" Patrick held his breath, wondering for a moment about what the woman had just said. *With what money?*

There was no time to wonder. Patrick realized that his family could have taken a train for who-knows-where, or they could be on their way up the river. "Did they say where they were going next?"

"I'm not sure. Your mother, brother, and sister were here for a few days," offered the woman, "searching for another relative, whom I do not believe they located."

"My grandfather?" Patrick wanted to be sure.

The woman nodded. "They left for Albury, farther upriver. Apparently, they heard a rumor they might find him there. I arranged their passage on the *Endeavor*."

"That's it, then," said Patrick, jumping up and down. "The *Endeavor*. Thank you."

Patrick was out the door in a second, with Jefferson on his heels. But something made him stop and turn around.

"Excuse me again," he said, poking his head back through the hotel's front door. "Did my father have red hair like mine, but curly?"

"Dark hair, I believe, and somewhat balding."

"Tall?"

"No, medium height, I suppose."

Patrick's heart sank. "Light, greenish brown?"

The man behind the counter was beginning to look embarrassed, and he put his hand to his cheek. "No, of that I'm certain. His eyes were quite distinctly dark, almost . . ."

"Jet black?" asked Jefferson.

Both the man and the woman nodded, but the puzzled look on their faces was back.

"That man was *not* my father," said Patrick, and he felt the back of his neck turn hot.

"But he specifically identified himself as John McWaid," said the woman. "Isn't that . . ."

Patrick sprinted out the door and back down the muddy street in the direction of the wharf.

"Wait a minute, Patrick." Jefferson stopped in front of a small brick building. "I still need to stop at the post office. I want to mail that letter to my cousins in Sydney."

"Do you really have to do that now?"

"There won't be another boat leaving tonight. What's your hurry?"

Jefferson stepped into the post office just as the woman inside came to the front door to lock up.

"Ma'am, just a quick letter, please?" Jefferson smiled sweetly at the woman, a trim lady in her fifties.

She sighed and stepped back to let them in.

"How long does it take for a letter to reach Sydney?" Jefferson asked her, scribbling a note on a piece of paper. "Can I send it to the post office there if I don't know the exact address?"

"You could try." The woman shook her head. "But Sydney is too big of a city now for that sort of thing. Not like Echuca." She waved toward a stack of small cubbyholes lining the far wall. "People here get mail without addresses all the time."

Jefferson nodded and finished his note, handing the woman a penny.

"I still can't believe Burke would tell them his name was McWaid," he told Patrick, who was waiting behind him. "What a pretender."

Before they turned to go, the postmistress looked curiously at the envelope Jefferson had addressed, then back at the boys.

"Pardon me," she asked them, "but did one of you say your name was McWaid?"

Patrick stopped at the door. "That's me. Patrick McWaid."

She smiled broadly and stabbed at the air as if she had just remembered something.

"I knew the name sounded familiar. Patrick McWaid. A letter just came in for you."

"Oh, it's not for me, I'm sure." Patrick shook his head. "No one knows I'm here. Not even my mother."

The woman narrowed her eyes at the boys the same way the people had at the hotel. "But your name *is* Patrick McWaid?"

"Yes, but . . ." Patrick had an uneasy feeling as he accepted the letter she held out to him. Sure enough, it *was* addressed to Patrick McWaid, Echuca, Victoria Territory. The handwriting even looked vaguely familiar, though it was faded. He turned the envelope over in his hands, but there was no name or return address on the back.

"Perhaps you should open it to see if it really is for you." The woman leaned forward and looked at the envelope curiously.

Patrick's hand shook as he hooked his thumb inside the corner of the flap and carefully ripped open the envelope.

"Is it for you?" The postmistress and Jefferson asked almost at the same time, but Patrick kept his attention focused on the letter.

Jefferson looked over his shoulder. "Dear Father?" he asked. "You're no father."

"Oh, dear," fretted the woman. "I feared it wasn't for you."

"Oh yes, it is," Patrick glanced up for a moment. "It's for me, thank you."

"What?" Jefferson tried to take the letter, but Patrick held it close and yanked his friend back out on the street with him.

"What's this all about?" Jefferson tried again to get another look. "It's—"

"It's for my grandfather." Patrick tried to keep his voice calm, but he could hardly read the letter, his hands were shaking so badly. "The grandfather I'm named after!"

Jefferson dropped his hands. "Why didn't you say so? Does that mean he really lives here in Echuca and just doesn't pick up his mail?"

Patrick shook his head. "I don't think so. Otherwise, the woman at the post office would have known about him."

"But who would have written your grandfather here in Echuca if he didn't live here?"

"My father." Patrick's voice cracked, and his head felt dizzy as he read and reread the letter. *Could it really be true?* "Can you believe it? My father wrote this letter."

Jefferson stopped to look at Patrick. "Let me see if I understand. First Burke comes to town and says he's your father. Now you have a letter to your long-lost grandfather from someone who also says he's your father. How do we know it's for real?"

"It's my father's handwriting." Patrick handed the letter to Jefferson. "See for yourself."

"I don't know your father's handwriting." But Jefferson's eyes grew wide as he read the note in the middle of the street.

"Didn't I tell you?" asked Patrick. "They tried to kill him on the prison ship, but he escaped."

"I can't believe it." Jefferson whistled through his teeth. "And now he's trying to come here because he thinks his father—"

"My grandfather."

"He thinks your grandfather can help him?"

"That's what it says." Patrick took the letter back and read it again. " 'I know you may not want to see me, and I cannot be sure this letter will ever reach you, but you are the only one to whom I can turn. . . .' "

Patrick walked in a daze down the middle of Pakenham Street on their way back down to the wharf. He clutched the letter tightly, as if the writing would bring him closer to his father.

This proves Pa is alive! Patrick would have danced down the street if he wasn't still upset at the news about how Burke was chasing his family and had probably even caught up to them.

A couple of men on horseback brushed by, almost knocking them over, but Patrick didn't care, lost in the thought of how his father had somehow escaped the people who had tried to hurt him. And now there was Conrad Burke to worry about.

"I know why he's here." Patrick was sure of himself this time. "If he gets to my ma, he'll get to my pa. There'll be no way for Pa to escape this time. He's the only one who knows the real truth about how criminal Burke and his friends really are."

"Wait a minute. You're talking about Burke now."

"Exactly."

"Patrick, your father isn't the only one who knows the truth. I thought you and Michael knew, too."

"We're just kids. No one believes us."

"I believe you. But we still have a problem."

Patrick jumped a puddle and landed on the wharf. "What's that?"

"We're out of money. I just spent my last penny on the letter."

CHAPTER 21

RIVER CHASE

Some dock workers passed Patrick and Jefferson as the men went home for the evening. A mosquito buzzed past Patrick's ear, and he swatted at it angrily.

"I didn't think we'd run out of money so soon," he sighed. "And we were so close."

Jefferson scratched his nose. "Well, I've been thinking. Want to know what I came up with?"

"What?"

"Nothing. You can pray all you want, but it won't change the fact that we have no money to live on."

Patrick stuffed the letter from his father into his pants pocket and sighed. His mother and Becky and Michael—and Burke—were hours ahead of them. But Jefferson had to be wrong. There *had* to be another way.

"Pardon me, boys" came the gruff voice Patrick had heard only a few times on the *Lady Elisabeth*. The Old Man stood at the top of the ladder to the wharf, trying to get by.

"I'm sorry." Patrick stepped aside to let the riverboat captain step past, but Jeff put up his hand.

"Sir, we're trying to catch up with Patrick's mother," he chirped. "You don't know when the next boat will be leaving, do you?"

"What?" The Old Man snapped to attention.

"Upriver. Patrick's family left on the *Endeavor*, and his mother doesn't even know Patrick is alive. We have to catch up with her before she disappears again."

The Old Man stared upriver. "What about your father?"

Almost before he knew what he was saying, Patrick spilled out a quick version of his father's story—being convicted of a crime he never committed, taken to Australia, and then having to run for his life.

Why am I telling him this? he wondered as he continued. Patrick even showed him the letter as proof.

The Old Man read it quietly and handed it back. "You'll want to save that letter," he told them. "Now you boys come with me." With a speed that surprised Patrick, the Old Man slid down the ladder and jumped across to the deck of the *Lady Elisabeth*.

"Kang Po," he shouted down into the hold of the boat. "Fire it back up. We're heading upriver right now!"

Kang Po shouted back a startled Chinese protest, but the Old Man brushed it aside.

"Fire it up now, or I'm coming in myself and doing the job!"

There was a silence for a moment, then a clattering and banging told them Kang Po was throwing wood into the fire. The Old Man looked back at Patrick and Jefferson.

"Are you coming?"

Patrick nearly bit his tongue. "Yes, sir!"

"Prentice! Prentice, are you sleeping again?" The captain prowled the salon, searching for his crew.

"Huh?" Prentice poked a sleepy head out from under a blanket in the corner of the room, and his eyes widened. "Captain, what are you doing back so soon?"

The Old Man crossed his arms. "We're getting under way as soon as Kang Po has steam up."

"But we have no supplies. You know we haven't even started to load—"

"Of course I know that!" thundered the Old Man. "But we're going upriver. Now, get dressed and untie this boat!"

From behind the Old Man, Patrick could only shrug when Prentice gave him a questioning look.

"Humph," grunted the Old Man as he turned to leave. "Crews these days. I want you two up on the bow, watching out for snags. Know what to look for? I don't want a log punching a hole in the hull."

Patrick nodded.

"All right, then. Where's my steam, Kang Po?" The Old Man left them to climb up his ladder as Patrick and Jefferson hurried to their new stations on the forward deck.

"I don't know what got into him," muttered Prentice, rubbing his eyes. "Maybe he's gone crazy."

"He's not crazy," said Patrick, looking up over his shoulder at the Old Man standing ready at the wheel of the *Lady Elisabeth*. Slowly, the paddle steamer pulled away from Echuca's wharf.

"Is that all the steam we have?" the Old Man shouted down from his perch. "Prentice, go help Kang Po. We can catch that old scow."

By "old scow," Patrick assumed the Old Man meant the *Endeavor*. And as long as they caught up with the boat soon, whatever the Old Man called it was fine with him.

Soon Prentice lit the bright running lamps, and they watched helplessly as branches and logs floated into the pool of light cast in front of them. Every time they saw a snag, he and Jefferson would wave their hands wildly and point, but usually it was too late to turn, and they tended to hit more river driftwood than they avoided.

"Ouch." Patrick winced. "That one hit hard. Maybe we ought to slow down."

But the Old Man didn't change the firm set of his chin, and Patrick was afraid to make any more suggestions, so he strained even harder to see into the night.

"This is absolutely insane," muttered Jefferson, but he kept his eyes on the river, too. "We could be doing this all night."

Patrick didn't mind. At least he was doing something, and his eyes were becoming used to the dark.

Three hours up the river, Patrick noticed something different floating in the water ahead of them. It wasn't a branch or a log.

"Hey!" yelled Patrick. "What's that?"

"I see it, too." Jefferson pointed at a piece of whitewashed, splintered wood.

Then came another piece and something that looked like a handrailing, only blackened.

"Looks as if they came off a ship." Jefferson sounded serious.

Prentice came up on the forward deck and stared into the night. Up behind the trees they could see a weak orange glow, sometimes flickering.

"Fire up ahead," called Prentice. He looked back to tell the captain, but the Old Man was already leaning out of the wheelhouse.

"If it's on the river," said the Old Man, "we may be picking up survivors."

Suddenly they changed from watching for logs to watching for people in the water, but Patrick didn't have time to even think of being afraid. They slowed down as they rounded the next bend. Before them was the charred, burning skeleton of a half-sunken riverboat that had once been very much like the *Lady Elisabeth*.

Patrick's mouth went dry, and he dug his fingernails into the railing.

"The *Endeavor*?" Patrick was afraid to know, but it had to be.

Lord, he prayed, without closing his eyes to the horrifying sight. *Where's Ma? And Becky and Michael?*

Prentice sprang to find a rope, and the *Lady Elisabeth* slowed to a crawl, paddling just enough to keep up with the current. The Old Man blew his whistle as Patrick ran back and forth along the railing, trying desperately to get a better view.

"There!" Jefferson was the first to spot a pair of survivors clinging to a snagged log on the far side of the channel, and they maneuvered over as close as they could.

"Can you catch the rope?" Prentice shouted into the night, but the two men on the log didn't move.

"I see more people over there," shouted the Old Man, gesturing in the opposite direction toward the wrecked riverboat.

Patrick knew they had to do something, and fast. Without a word he ran to the dark back end of the *Lady Elisabeth*, where the ship's rowboat was stored on deck.

"It's too big," he grunted, trying to shove it off the side into the river.

"There you go, trying to be a hero again." Jefferson appeared next to him.

"I'm not a hero. Why don't you help me get it into the water?" Patrick shoved his shoulder into the side of the boat and pushed once more.

Jefferson sighed and pushed, and the rowboat landed in the river with a splash. Patrick caught his breath when he realized what he was doing. A little boat on the river . . .

He clenched his hands into fists. *There's no time to be afraid of the water.*

"I'm coming with you," Jefferson said.

"Not enough room," argued Patrick. Before Jefferson could stop him or he could change his mind, Patrick closed his eyes and tumbled into the boat by himself. Quickly, he locked the oars into place and rowed swiftly for the survivors. A moment later he was around the *Lady Elisabeth* and close by the snag.

"What are you doing out there?" yelled Prentice.

"I'll pick these people up," Patrick yelled back. "Go get the others."

Prentice looked up at the Old Man for instructions, and the paddle steamer pulled away.

"Are you there?" Patrick yelled into the dark. He could barely make out the snag in the flickering light from the still-burning hulk.

"Here!" came a weak voice, almost right next to him.

"Can you climb aboard?" asked Patrick. "I can hold the boat."

No one answered, but someone was groaning.

"Climb up!" Patrick was having trouble keeping his boat next to the snag against the current. "I'm here to help."

"My friend's hurt badly," said a young man, then someone grabbed the front of the boat.

"Careful," Patrick warned. "Don't tip us over."

With a little help the man was able to roll into the front of the boat, where he lay shivering, while Patrick helped a second man feel his way to the stern. Even in the shadows Patrick could see the second fellow's clothes were burned and charred.

"Are you all right?" gasped Patrick as he tugged him into the boat like a giant fish.

The second man said nothing, only sat with his face in his hands.

"Galley fire got out of control," explained the first. "He tried to put it out, but it got away from us. Next thing we knew, the whole ship was on fire."

With their little boat weighed down almost to the edge, Patrick slipped back to his place at the oars and pulled for the lights on the other side of the river.

"Was there a Mrs. McWaid on your ship?" he asked.

"Dunno. Could have been."

Patrick sighed and rowed harder.

Once they had the two survivors safely on board the *Lady Elisabeth*, Patrick could see that the Old Man had nudged his ship up to the bank, a safe distance from the ruined *Endeavor*. Their salon had turned into a makeshift hospital to treat the cold and frightened people.

"My mother!" Patrick shook Jefferson's arm as they helped an older woman find a blanket. "Have you seen my mother? Or Becky?"

Jefferson shook his head. "Sorry, Patrick. I already asked. Someone just told me your ma and Becky ran off." He pointed down the river. "That way."

"What?" Patrick ran to the railing and stared into the night. "Why would they do that?"

"They said—" began Jefferson, but Patrick was already on the run.

"Ma!" he shouted. He scanned the narrow strip of muddy river beach for signs of his family, but all he saw were two sets of foot-prints leading into the thick overhanging trees. When he jumped out to follow, he sank up to his ankles in mud.

"Heard tell there were sixteen on board when it caught fire." Jefferson followed a few steps behind. "I counted twelve, so there are still four people out there."

Ma, Becky, and Michael make three, Patrick figured. *And Burke . . .*

"Ma!" Patrick yelled himself hoarse, and they followed the foot-steps in the mud until they could see them no longer. "Becky!"

He slashed his way through a tangle of bushes, not feeling the sting of the branches cutting his arms. "But why would they leave everyone else?"

Jefferson put his hand on Patrick's shoulder. "The others told me they went off to find Michael."

"Michael? Wasn't he with them?"

"I've been trying to tell you, Patrick. He disappeared soon as the fire started."

Now Patrick moved faster and yelled more loudly. A half-moon hung over the trees, helping them to see better. But the going was slow through the thick bushes and swampy ponds by the riverbank.

"How far could they have come?" wondered Jefferson as Patrick continued yelling into the night. Finally, when their way was blocked by yet another swamp, they both stood still.

"There," said Jefferson after a moment. "Did you hear that?

Patrick wasn't sure, but he shouted once again. "Ma!"

Patrick was the first to see the two figures wading slowly in waist-deep water along the edge of the river. He knew who they were in an instant and ran out into the water to meet them.

"Patrick, is it really you?" Mrs. McWaid's voice was nearly gone. "How can it be?"

"It *is* me, Ma, it really is." Patrick put his arms around his mother and sister while Jefferson gave them a hand up to higher ground. "And Jefferson, too."

Becky gasped as if she had seen a ghost.

"But we thought you were both . . ." Becky couldn't finish, and their mother hugged them and sobbed, not letting go.

"Patrick," she managed to whisper at last. She held her son at arm's length and studied his face. "You have to explain what happened."

"They had a funeral for you on the ship." Becky let the tears run down her cheeks.

"I know." Patrick nodded. "I'll tell you what happened, but it's a long story."

"We should get back to the paddle steamer," added Jefferson.

"I still can't believe it." Mrs. McWaid pinched her son's cheek and looked into his eyes.

"But, Ma, what about Michael?" Patrick pulled them along. "We have to find him."

"Everything happened so fast," Becky answered for her mother. "The last thing we remember is seeing Mr. Burke carrying Michael and Christopher, and then they were gone."

"Christopher?" Jefferson sounded confused.

"Someone in Echuca gave Michael an orphaned baby koala bear," explained Becky as they hurried back to where the *Lady Elisabeth* sat waiting. "He's been carrying it everywhere."

Patrick hit his fist against the palm of his hand. "So Burke has Michael. I can't believe it."

"We searched as far as we could," sighed Mrs. McWaid. She tried to catch her breath as they climbed aboard. "Perhaps they're on the other side of the river."

"They would have yelled back if they could," answered Patrick. "Don't you think?"

"We can search more river from the *Lady Elisabeth*," suggested Jefferson, helping Becky step up to the deck. "The Old Man will know what to do."

Becky and her mother were quickly introduced to the Old Man, who sadly surveyed the wreck of the *Endeavor* one last time.

"More lanterns now, Prentice," he ordered, leaning out his window in the wheelhouse. "We're going to search the river until we find this lad."

CHAPTER 22

DARKNESS LIKE DAYLIGHT

Patrick looked around the crowded salon. A couple of the survivors from the *Endeavor* were propped up in chairs, but the man he had rescued in the rowboat was probably the most seriously hurt.

"Can't we fill up some more of these lanterns?" asked Jefferson.

Prentice frowned and pulled at his thinning gray hair. "We don't have any more kerosene, I'm afraid. Burned it in the boilers, remember?"

Patrick remembered the race a few days ago and groaned.

"All we have are the two deck lights," said Jefferson.

"It doesn't matter." Patrick marched out on deck and stared hard at the riverbank as they drifted past the spot where they had met up with his mother and Becky. "We'll still find Michael."

But as Patrick and the others leaned over the railing in the darkness, Patrick wasn't sure he could believe his own words.

"It's so dark," whispered his sister. "Can you see anything?"

Patrick bit his lip until it hurt, afraid to talk, afraid to do anything that would keep him from finding his brother.

"It reminds me of being in the cave," Jefferson whispered.

"Uh-huh."

"Remember your verse about darkness turning into daylight?"

"You're thinking about that *now*?"

"I admit I thought it was silly at the time. But now . . ."

"It would be nice," Patrick finished his friend's thought, remembering the cave and how much he had wanted God to light up the darkness. Just like then, he would do anything now for a ray of sunshine, and he prayed quietly.

"Are you praying, Patrick?"

Jefferson's question didn't surprise him this time.

"Yes."

"Well, you'd better pray harder, then, because one of the deck lights just went out."

Patrick was afraid to look up, but Jefferson was right. One by one, the lamps left inside the *Lady Elisabeth* were blinking out, also. Ten minutes later, the second and last deck searchlight flickered. For a few moments all they had was moonlight.

"The Old Man can make it back to Echuca in his sleep." Prentice appeared on deck with a dim, sputtering hand-held lantern, spilling barely more light than a candle. "I'm sorry, but we'd better try searching again in the morning when it's light."

They could still hear his mother's shouts on the other side of the boat.

"No!" Patrick nearly screamed back. Panic made him shake. "We can't give up. The Old Man *promised* we would find Michael!"

"But . . ." Prentice said sadly, then handed the last flickering flame to Patrick. "All right, then. This lamp has almost run dry, too. But at least it has a reflector."

His mother and Becky joined them. "The moon's not helping much anymore," Mrs. McWaid told them. "Too many clouds."

"I know!" Jefferson piped up. "Isn't there something from the galley we could use for torches? Bacon grease and rags? Anything?"

"Good idea," answered Prentice, "but the galley is bare. We didn't have time to stock up in Echuca."

Patrick waved his feeble lantern out over the side while the paddle steamer slowly made its way back toward Echuca. Everyone was quiet, except for the calls that echoed up and down the river. Here and there a star peeked around the clouds, and for a second Patrick thought he saw the reflection of the Southern Cross on the water.

"Mi-chael!" Jefferson took turns calling.

Patrick had no voice left. In the dim light he could see his mother and Becky beside him. He hadn't realized how worn and muddy they looked until now.

"Michael," Patrick tried again. A pair of golden yellow eyes—animal eyes—caught the last weak flicker of his lamp just before it went out.

"Did you see that?" cried Patrick.

"Just an animal, son." Prentice sounded like a kindly grandfather.

"Stop!" Patrick shouted up to the Old Man. "Please stop the boat!"

"Patrick, it was just a pair of critter eyes you saw," Prentice tried to convince him. "I saw them, too."

"There was more." Patrick hadn't actually *seen* anything else, but he couldn't let it pass. Already the *Lady Elisabeth* was drifting past the place where he had seen the yellow eyes. He ran back along the deck, vaulted over the paddle wheel box, and pushed by two *Endeavor* passengers. The lantern in his hand caught on a corner of the boat, shattering glass into the river, but he didn't care. He did pull his father's letter out of his back pocket, though, throwing it to the deck as he ran.

"Michael!"

Without another thought he was in the water again, just as he had been when Jefferson needed help. The old fear had shattered like the lamp. And this time there was someone beside him, swimming powerfully.

"I saw him, too," said the Old Man.

The current was stronger than Patrick realized, pushing at him from the direction he most wanted to go.

"Cut across," the Old Man instructed, and Patrick could feel the man's hand brush up against his elbow. Straight ahead he could barely make out the branches of a snag, just behind the last bend in the river.

"Are you all right?" the captain asked.

Patrick's arms were growing numb, but he managed to mumble

that he was fine. The snag was just ahead. The way it was hidden, it was no wonder they hadn't seen it on the way up.

In the branches of a floating tree—or rather in its upturned roots—they could see something moving. A patch of white, two big ears, and then the glow of two enormous, scared eyes.

"Koala," said the Old Man. "But that's not what I saw. Michael?"

They heard a faint whimper. Patrick was closest; he reached into the gnarled mess and felt a shirt. *Michael!*

"We found him!" bellowed the Old Man in the direction of the *Lady Elisabeth*. "For goodness sake, Prentice, would you bring the boat over here?"

CHAPTER 23

YOU KNOW THE TRUTH

Wrapped in wonderfully warm and scratchy wool blankets back on the *Lady Elisabeth*, Michael and his koala were the center of attention all the way back to Echuca. His mother rubbed the life back into his pale arms and legs while the McWaids huddled next to the boiler for extra warmth.

"But, Ma," he objected through chattering teeth. "We're scaring poor Christopher."

The koala had looked as excited as a koala could as Patrick had helped to dry the kitten-sized creature, wrapping him in a blanket in a warm corner of the cramped boiler room.

"It's all the noise," suggested Becky.

"Poor Christopher is not my first concern right now, dear Michael," said their mother as she hovered over her youngest. "My first concern is holding on to you and your brother. You are not leaving my sight ever again, not even for a second."

Kang Po stepped past them and opened the boiler to throw in another piece of split red gumwood. The golden light from the fire played on their faces.

"Oh!" Becky crossed her arms and shivered. "I hope I never see Conrad Burke again in my life!"

"Me neither," chimed in Michael. "I knew he was lying about helping us find our grandpa."

"It wasn't your fault, dear," replied their mother. "We all knew. We just couldn't do anything about him following us."

"Did he . . ." Patrick was afraid to ask if Burke had drowned in the river. And had he really been trying to help Michael, or kidnap him?

Becky answered his unasked question. "I don't know what happened to him."

"All I know is that when the boat caught fire, he grabbed me." Michael shook his head. "Then your boat came, and he let me go and swam away. It was dark."

"The captain said they would go back and search the area in the daylight," reminded their mother. Patrick noticed she was holding his father's letter. "If Mr. Burke is alive, they'll find him in the morning. I'm just glad I have all three of you safe now."

"But how did you know it was Michael out in the river?" Becky asked Patrick.

"I wasn't sure." Patrick warmed his hands next to the boiler. "I just saw the light in the koala's eyes, and I had a feeling Michael was there, too."

Patrick knew that sounded odd, but he also knew his prayer had been answered—the prayer about a light in the darkness.

Becky looked as if she didn't quite understand. "Well, as soon as you jumped in, the captain yelled at Mr. Prentice to steer. He dived right in after you."

Patrick nodded. "I didn't see Michael until we were at the snag. It was the Old Man who saw him first."

"What a horrible name," said Becky. "The Old Man? What's his real name?"

"I don't know. Not even Prentice knows."

"You're right about that." Jefferson was leaning against the doorway, barely visible in the soft glow from the boiler. "But now promise me one thing, Irishman."

"If I can."

"No more jumping into the water. You proved whatever you were trying to prove. Twice is more than enough, and that's the truth."

Patrick let himself laugh, as much at what Jefferson said as at the sight of the baby koala crawling up on Michael's shoulders.

"Sure enough, that's the truth, Jeff." His own words reminded him of something his father had told him in the prison in Dublin. *You know the truth, Patrick. Don't forget the truth!*

"We're going to find Pa, little one," Patrick whispered to the koala as he stroked the animal on the head. "I know we will."

AUSTRALIA AS IT REALLY WAS

During the late 1700s and early 1800s, conditions in English jails were horrible and overcrowded. Prisoners, many of them Irish, were often given seven- or ten-year sentences for things like stealing sheep or breaking a window. Today we might think that punishment sounds harsh, and maybe it was. At the same time, other prisoners were dangerous criminals, even murderers. What could the English do with so many prisoners?

Let's send them all far away, someone suggested. We'll put them to work, and at the same time they can help us tame a great, desolate land—the English colony of Australia. That's how the prisoners sentenced to "Transportation" to Australia became part of a giant experiment, and between 1788 and 1868, some 160,000 prisoners were taken by ship from England to Australia.

The last prison ship, the *Hougoumont*, delivered its final cargo of prisoners to Western Australia in 1868. Many of those prisoners were Irishmen convicted of "Fenianism," or being part of an illegal group called the "Fenians" that wanted Ireland to be independent from England.

That much is real history. *Escape to Murray River* asks a few more questions: What would happen if one of those prisoners really hadn't done anything wrong? Worse yet, what if an innocent person was set up by the real criminals to make it look as if he *had* done something wrong? In 1867, he might have been sent to Western Australia, just like in our story. This remote outpost was the perfect place to bring prisoners. The area needed workers because there was a lot of hard work to do, and few people wanted to come there on their own. The area was barren and dry and so far away from anywhere else that there was no way of escape—without a little help.

But one real-life prisoner actually did make a daring escape on a ship chartered by Irish-American friends. He was a well-known Irish writer named John Boyle O'Reilly. Of course, there's no record of his children coming to help him, or even any evidence that he was innocent of the crime that got him sent to Australia in the first place. But no matter. There's plenty of other fascinating history we know about from that time, even beyond the story of the prisoners.

Australia's gold rush, for instance, brought thousands of treasure seekers to the colony in the 1850s. Settlers from all over the world would follow, discovering places like the beautiful Murray River Valley, Kangaroo Island, and the eastern coast.

As they arrived, many pioneers started farms or sheep and cattle ranches, and paddle steamers began sailing up and down Australia's largest river system, the Murray. Some, like Patrick and Becky McWaid, brought their strong faith in God as they faced the challenges of an untamed land. Making their way to the booming river town of Echuca, these pioneers would find plenty of adventures "Down Under."

A special thanks to these Australians . . .

Murray Johnson of Echuca, Victoria, who loves the river and whose encouragement has helped in many ways.

Norman Millner of the Signal Point Interpretive Center in Goolwa, South Australia, for reviewing portions of the manuscript.

Neil Waller of the Kangaroo Island Pioneers Association, for firsthand accounts of the island.

And the helpful staff at the Victor Harbor Tourist Information Center, South Australia. Thank you!

From the Author

One of the best parts about writing is hearing back from readers. Do you have any questions or just want to let me know what you thought of the books? Please feel free to drop me a line, care of Bethany House Publishers, 11300 Hampshire Avenue South, Minneapolis, Minnesota, 55438.

Robert Elmer

Series for Middle Graders*
From Bethany House Publishers

ADVENTURES DOWN UNDER · by Robert Elmer
When Patrick McWaid's father is unjustly sent to Australia as a prisoner in 1867, the rest of the family follows, uncovering action-packed mystery along the way.

ADVENTURES OF THE NORTHWOODS · by Lois Walfrid Johnson
Kate O'Connell and her stepbrother Anders encounter mystery and adventure in northwest Wisconsin near the turn of the century.

AN AMERICAN ADVENTURE SERIES · by Lee Roddy
Hildy Corrigan and her family must overcome danger and hardship during the Great Depression as they search for a "forever home."

BLOODHOUNDS, INC. · by Bill Myers
Hilarious, hair-raising suspense follows brother-and-sister detectives Sean and Melissa Hunter in these madcap mysteries with a message.

JOURNEYS TO FAYRAH · by Bill Myers
Join Denise, Nathan, and Josh on amazing journeys as they discover the wonders and lessons of the mystical Kingdom of Fayrah.

MANDIE BOOKS · by Lois Gladys Leppard
With over four million sold, the turn-of-the-century adventures of Mandie and her many friends will keep readers eager for more.

THE RIVERBOAT ADVENTURES · by Lois Walfrid Johnson
Libby Norstad and her friend Caleb face the challenges and risks of working with the Underground Railroad during the mid–1800s.

TRAILBLAZER BOOKS · by Dave and Neta Jackson
Follow the exciting lives of real-life Christian heroes through the eyes of child characters as they share their faith and God's love with others around the world.

THE TWELVE CANDLES CLUB · by Elaine L. Schulte
When four twelve-year-old girls set up a business doing odd jobs and baby-sitting, they find themselves in the midst of wacky adventures and hilarious surprises.

THE YOUNG UNDERGROUND · by Robert Elmer
Peter and Elise Andersen's plots to protect their friends and themselves from Nazi soldiers in World War II Denmark guarantee fast-paced action and suspenseful reads.

*(ages 8–13)